Entangled Realities

Also by Kim Antieau

Novels
The Blue Tale • *Broken Moon* • *Church of the Old Mermaids*
Coyote Cowgirl • *Deathmark* • *The Fish Wife* • *The Gaia Websters*
Her Frozen Wild • *The Jigsaw Woman*
Mercy, Unbound • *Ruby's Imagine* • *Swans in Winter*

Nonfiction
Counting on Wildflowers: An Entanglement • *The Salmon Mysteries: A
Guidebook to a Reimagining of the Eleusinian Mysteries*

Short Story Collections
Trudging to Eden • *The First Book of Old Mermaids Tales*
Tales Fabulous and Fairy

Chapbook
Blossoms

Blog
www.kimantieau.com

Also by Mario Milosevic

Novels
Terrastina and Mazolli: a Novel in 99-Word Episodes • *Kyle's War*
Claypot Dreamstance • *The Last Giant* • *The Coma Monologues*

Short Novel
The Doctor and the Clown

Short Story Collection
Miniatures

Poetry
Animal Life • *Fantasy Life* • *Love Life*

Blog
mariowrites.com

Entangled Realities

short fiction by

Kim Antieau
&
Mario Milosevic

Green Snake
PUBLISHING

Entangled Realities
by Kim Antieau and Mario Milosevic

Copyright © 2012 by Kim Antieau and Mario Milosevic

ISBN: 978-1-949644-50-0

All Rights Reserved.

Original publication of these stories as follows:
   "Hauntings," *Asimov's,* February 1985
   "Up Above the World So High," *The Clarion Awards*, 1984
   "Sanctuary," *Shadows 9,* 1986
   "Winding Broomcorn," *Fantasy & Science Fiction*, February 2009
   "Listening for the General," *Twilight Zone Magazine*, February 1988
   "The Untied States of America," *Interzone*, May/June 2010

Cover © Hui Sima | Dreamstime.com
Book design by Mario Milosevic
Special thanks to Ruth Ford Biersdorf

No part of this book may be reproduced
without written permission of the authors.

Electronic editions of this book
are available at most e-book stores.

Published by Green Snake Publishing
www.greensnakepublishing.com

www.kimantieau.com

mariowrites.com

For our parents:

Mary Antieau
Agica Milosevic
Lloyd Antieau
Ilija Milosevic

Contents

Introduction

We're a writing couple. This means we spend a lot of our time alone in our imaginations, inventing characters, settings, and plots for our amusement and—we hope—for the amusement of our readers. We've both been writing since we were children, and maybe even before that, before we had language.

Kim started telling stories with pictures before she could read or write. Mario must have been wanting to write from a young age because he remembers his parents getting him a typewriter when he was nine years old. He learned to write on it and began submitting stories to magazines a few years later when he was in his early teens.

We also read a lot, which we think is the best training for

any writer: read, read, read. Mario loved science fiction and inhaled all the books he could find by Isaac Asimov, Arthur C. Clarke, and all the other golden age writers. Sometimes he read two books a day. Kim loved fairy tales, history books, and horse books, but she also read many classics as a child.

We met in 1980 at Michigan State University where we were both attending a writing workshop. Mario was from Canada; this was his first time in the United States. Kim was raised in Michigan, so East Lansing was her backyard. For both of us, the workshop felt simultaneously alien and comfortable. Alien because it was the first time either of us could devote six uninterrupted weeks to our writing. And comfortable because we were surrounded by other workshop participants who had come to devote themselves to writing, too.

We had found our tribe.

We both admired each other's writing right away. Mario was impressed by Kim's ability to create extraordinarily believable characters and place them in fully realized worlds. He admired her talent for realistic dialogue and her pure storytelling abilities. Kim was taken with Mario's bizarre and quirky imagination. She liked how he often found the oblique and surrealist angle in everyday life.

By the end of the workshop, we were a bona fide couple. Less than a year later, we got married on a beautiful Sunday afternoon in a park in Ann Arbor with both of our families attending.

We were a writing couple from the start: For wedding gifts we asked for writing paper, typewriter ribbons, and postage for mailing manuscripts. Our friends and family obliged our

    KIM ANTIEAU and MARIO MILOSEVIC

wishes, although some were a little confused. Manila envelopes to start our wedded life? Yup.

Here it is more than thirty years later, and we haven't looked back. We kept writing our stories, novels, and poems and mailing them to magazines and publishers. Sometimes they got accepted. Mostly they came back. We learned to roll with the ups and downs of the writing life. We took day jobs, as many writers do, and kept working at our craft, kept telling stories.

We've had a successful life collaboration, but one thing we've always had difficulty doing is finding a way to collaborate on a piece of writing. We've tried a few times, but our thought processes—the way we approach story and language—are so different that we have not been able to write a story together.

We did collaborate very well on a project in the nineties when we co-published *Daughters of Nyx: A Magazine of Goddess Stories, Mythmaking, and Fairy Tales.* Kim was the editor and Mario was the production guy. Kim found contributing writers and artists for the magazine and worked with them on their stories and illustrations. Mario read the slush and did the production work on the magazine. Together we produced seven beautiful issues of the magazine until economic reality set in, and we had to end the run.

Producing *Daughters of Nyx* was not a writing collaboration, but it was a creative collaboration we both enjoyed. All the skills we learned served us well when we started Green Snake Publishing. Mario does the production work for the POD and ebooks. Kim takes photographs for our covers and is great at scrounging up other images for our covers from various sources. We work together on the design of our books. Of course, we both write stories and books for the company.

We're both proud of the books we have produced and feel like this is another successful area of collaboration for us.

Which brings us to this book, our first writing collaboration of a sort. Maybe we can't co-write anything, but we can be in a book together. We each picked three of our favorite stories—Kim picked Mario's and Mario picked Kim's—and we put them into *Entangled Realities.*

In "Hauntings," Kim imagines a woman living alone in a house that appears to be haunted, only these ghosts are very particular about who they are haunting. The story originally appeared in *Asimov's SF* and has been reprinted several times. Kim got the idea for the story after she traveled to Arizona and explored the Betatakin ruins. After "Hauntings" appeared, she expanded it into the novel *Ruins,* which is not yet published.

"Up Above the World So High" by Mario takes its title from a famous children's rhyme. The two teenage girls in the story have spent their entire lives on a wooden sailing ship that never docks or touches land. Mario conceived the story as a kind of winking nod to science fiction tales of generation spaceships. The story is a poignant look at the cost of friendship and what it takes to survive in any time or place. It was Mario's first major sale. Damon Knight bought it for his anthology *The Clarion Awards.*

Survival is also at the core of Kim's story "Sanctuary." The young man in the tale finds out that a young woman in town never leaves her house. He decides to "cure" her of her af-

   KIM ANTIEAU and MARIO MILOSEVIC

fliction. This story takes place in Canyons, a fictional town in Kim's universe which is a lot like the coastal town of Bandon, where we lived for four years. Kim was inspired to write this story after she had a bout of agoraphobia. Charles L. Grant published it in his *Shadows* anthology series.

"Winding Broomcorn," a recent story of Mario's from *The Magazine of Fantasy and Science Fiction*, concerns what happens when a strange woman comes to an old widower's house and asks him if he will make a broom for her. Mario got the idea for the story when he was working for *Ruralite* magazine, and he interviewed a man who makes brooms from the broomcorn he grows himself.

"Listening for the General" by Kim was inspired by the poem "The Colonel," written by Carolyn Forché. In the poem Forché describes meeting with a warlord who keeps ears in a paper sack like so many dried peach halves. The image of the ears sparked Kim's tale of an old woman who is determined to bring down a warlord with her knowledge of the old ways. Kim tried to use sound as the main sensory experience throughout the entire story. She wrote this during the time we were involved in the peace movement and working on the periphery of the Sanctuary movement and trying to help the people of El Salvador. "Listening for the General" originally appeared in *The Twilight Zone Magazine*.

"The Untied States of America" by Mario ends this collection with a gentle tale of the breakup of the country. Mario got the idea for the story when he realized that transposing two letters in "united" turns the word into its opposite: "untied." He wrote the story some years ago, then forgot about it and recently found it on his hard drive and sent it off to *Interzone* which published it in 2010, a particularly turbulent time in our country's history. The story was named one of the best of the year by *Locus* magazine and won Mario a grant from the Speculative Literature Foundation.

Sometimes stories are hard to get on paper, other times they seem to flow out with almost no effort from us at all. When the flow is going well, it can seem like we're just stenographers to the muses, taking dictation as fast as we can.

Those are the best times. That's when we feel like we are plugged into some divine spark of the Universe. That spark can cleanse, heal, and sustain us as nothing else can.

We have a favorite quote that we never tire of repeating or hearing. It's by Muriel Rukeyser from her long poem "The Speed of Dark," and it goes like this: "The universe is made of stories, not atoms."

We both find meaning and hope in stories and in the telling of stories, even in tales with unhappy endings. So here are some stories from our universe, a universe that is definitely made up of stories.

Enjoy!

Kim Antieau & Mario Milosevic

March, 2012

Hauntings
Kim Antieau

Kate awakened to the sound of her name being whispered in her ear, to the feel of warm breath on her cheek. She let the dream ebb away, taking with it the sound and warmth before she opened her eyes to darkness.

"Kate," the whisperer said again, sighing, settling and creaking as all houses do in the quiet of night.

Still not fully awake, Kate switched on the light over her bed. Eerie shadows gave way to reveal her ordinary bedroom: faded peach wallpaper, painted ceramic light fixtures, jeans and shirt strewn on a chair, a black and white television set. The sound was gone.

She took a drink of water from the glass that was always

on the night stand. She drank a great deal of water now, as if it could wash her clean if she drank enough of it. She yawned and settled back against her pillow. The whispering didn't frighten her. She had grown accustomed to the occasional noises in the two weeks she had lived in the nineteenth century farmhouse. They were almost company to her.

Except now they were disturbing her sleep even more than usual. She liked her time in her dreams. In them, she was usually well, whole; no one had taken a knife to her, no one had injected poisons into her.

She turned the light off. In the morning, she supposed, she'd have to find out why the house talked to her.

"Can I help you find anything, Mrs. Hein?" the librarian asked. Kate looked up and smiled. Everyone in Canyons insisted on calling her Mrs. even though her last name was different from her husband's. All they knew was that she was married, so she was Mrs. Hein to them.

"Call me Kate, please," Kate said, closing the book in front of her. "Maybe you can help. Do you know anything about the Nelson farmhouse?"

"You mean the house you bought?" he asked, sitting down next to her. On this sunny Monday afternoon, the library was empty except for Kate and the librarian. "It's been researched extensively by our historical society—of which I am a member. It hasn't been declared a historical landmark or anything— not architecturally unique enough—but it is one of our older homes. The society has pictures of it and of the people who lived in it. Their office is just across the courtyard."

"Before I bought it had the Nelsons always owned it?"

He shook his head. "It was built by a family from back east in the 1890s. They had money and decided to come here and get back to nature."

"People were doing that back then, too, eh?" Kate said, laughing. One of the reasons she had moved to Canyons was because there was no industry, no waste dumps, and plenty of land to grow her own food.

"I can't remember their names, something simple though," he said. "They owned it for about fifty years. Then they sold it to a distant cousin and moved back to New York. This cousin married a Nelson and it stayed in their family after that. They over-farmed the land, though, and they couldn't make any money, so they finally left. It was up for sale two years before you bought it."

"Any rumors of unusual happenings?" Kate asked.

The librarian glanced at her books *Poltergeists* and *Hauntings*.

"Nary a word," he said, "and I would have heard. It seems it was quite a happy home."

"Any Indian burial grounds nearby?"

The librarian laughed and stood up. "Nope. We didn't have Indians in that area. You're going to have to settle with just your run-of-the-mill ordinary house."

"Thanks." She turned back to her stack of books and magazines, and he went back to the check-out counter. Leafing through one of the magazines, the headline "Laetrile: Hope of the Future" caught her attention. She quickly turned the page. She never wanted to see another cancer article. When she had first found out she had cancer, she had read them all—after the initial frightened vomiting ended and the terrified night sweats lessened in frequency. For a time, she had thought about going the "natural" route, healing with foods and state of mind. In the end, she decided she couldn't trust her mind not to make the disease worse, so she had allowed surgery and chemotherapy.

She pushed away from the table and quickly left the library. Anger whirled around her as she stepped into the sunshine; the anger swelled in her and turned into fear. They said she was free of cancer now. What did they know? In twenty years when she was just over fifty, she would probably get cancer from the chemo and have to go through it all over again. She shivered and pulled the sweater closer to her. The house. She had to concentrate on the house. She crossed the courtyard and went toward the historical society office.

"Can I come for a visit soon?" Jeff asked over the phone. "It's been two weeks, Katie. I miss you."

"I thought you had an assignment," Kate said. She pulled the long telephone cord around with her as she walked from one end of the huge farm kitchen to the other. It was an uneconomical space, but the painted blue walls and the Dutch ceramic tiles made her feel cozy. The white cupboards stretched to the ceiling and Kate envisioned shelf upon shelf of Kerr canning jars filled with peaches, apples, tomatoes.

"Winter has set in there early this year," Jeff said, "so they cancelled it until spring."

"Spring?" Kate said, taking the tea kettle off the burner.

The piercing whistle slowly hiccoughed to a stop. "That's six months."

"Yeah," he said. "Maybe by then you'll want to come back to work. Hint, hint."

Kate stopped moving. "I'm through, Jeff. Period. I like it here." There was silence on the other end. "Whatsamatter, don't you like your new partner?" she joked.

"He's not fun to cuddle with and he's not my partner," he said. "You and I are still under contract."

That much was true; they owed their publisher three books. She had been writing the texts and Jeff had been taking the photographs for their travel books since before they left college. They had just started branching out into more naturalistic settings (versus tourist spots) when Kate had gotten sick.

"I love you," he said. He sighed. "If you still need time alone, I understand."

She bit the inside of her cheek so she wouldn't cry. They had never been apart for this long, and even though it was her choice and it was temporary, she missed him.

"Come this weekend," she said.

Kate liked the house. In some ways it reminded her of her childhood—though when she really thought about it, she knew it was her father's childhood it reminded her of. She didn't want to think about her own past. What she had believed had been an idyllic child's life now seemed tainted with all the things that should have been done: Her parents should have fed her better foods, they shouldn't have put her through the stress of a custody battle when she was a teenager, and they should have known they lived two miles from the most toxic waste dump in the state. She leaned back in the chair, stretching her legs across the table. It made her too angry, the past, because there was not a thing she could do about it. It was just a compilation of "ifs".

The house shifted, and Kate let all thoughts of her past slip away. It was the house's past she was interested in now. The library and the historical society had not given her any clues as to why the house made noises; perhaps the house itself could.

"The attic," she said, dropping her feet from the coffee table and standing up. She glanced out the window at the fading light, wondering if she wanted to go into the attic at night, especially the attic of a haunted house. Heroines of horror novels were often doing things just like this and she'd always thought they were a bit stupid. She laughed; the sound vibrated around her, as if the walls were enjoying the sound. Kate was not afraid of the house, and she was not a heroine.

The attic was brightly lit by a line of fluorescent lights a previous owner had installed. Except for a work table and several boxes strewn in different corners, the room was empty. What little there was of Kate's things was still downstairs. Between buying the house and maintaining an apartment in the city, they had had little money left over for her to buy furnishings.

Kate knelt on the floor and began examining the boxes. Two of them were filled with moth-eaten clothes. Another box contained homemade Christmas decorations.

"Bingo," Kate said as she opened the last box and began

taking out papers. Twenty-year-old grocery and utility bills. She dug deeper and found several letters. All were newsy, chatty letters from relatives asking the Nelsons about their rural life. At the bottom of the box were three letters written by Agatha Nelson to Aunt Betty Carens which had never been mailed: "The new calf is doing better. . . . We need rain. . . . The cows got loose in the alfalfa patch and gorged themselves." Folded in with Agatha's third letter was a faded page written in someone else's hand: '. . . Look what I found in the attic," Agatha had written. "Nellie Smith was one of the original owners. Please return this to me . . ."

Smiths and Nelsons. The all-American farmhouse. Nellie Smith's letter was like a piece of a diary, addressed to no one in particular. She described the farm and then the house: "The house is completed now, and we are settled in. I love it here away from the city. It is still in this house as if there is no past or future, just now—or as if it were all one time and what happened or will does not matter . . ."

Kate smiled and tucked the letter into her pocket to show to Jeff later. Perhaps one day she would develop Nellie's philosophy and none of it would matter to her either. She switched off the lights and went down the stairs.

"You're too ordinary," Kate said. "Maybe that's why you're haunted."

She brought herbal tea and peanut butter cookies up to her bedroom and turned on a romantic comedy from the fifties. She skimmed through the book on hauntings. It told her nothing new. Dead people haunted houses. Period.

She snapped the book shut and opened the one on poltergeists. They were usually short-term phenomena revolving around one person, often a troubled adolescent. It had not occurred to her that she could be causing the sounds, that perhaps it was all in her head. She was not a troubled teenager, but she was not a particularly happy adult.

When Kate awakened that night, the only noise she heard was coming from the marsh pond over her back hill. She sat up and drank from her glass. The clock read 2:45.

Feeling irritable, Kate got out of bed and went downstairs. She had not slept through an entire night in nearly two years.

She took an orange from the refrigerator and went into the living room and sank into her chair. Through the open curtains, she could see the back yard, touched with a bit of fairyland by the moonlight. "Kate," the room whispered.

Kate sat up straight and looked around the room. It was bathed in a white glow—moonlight—and something else in the middle of the room. Shimmering half there and half not was a woman. Kate blinked. The woman appeared to be sitting, her arms outstretched, her hands flat against something. Her image wavered, and Kate thought she saw someone else sitting, next to her. The image faded and was gone.

Kate sat very still for a long while. When the clock chimed four, she went back upstairs.

The next morning, Kate was still not frightened, and it puzzled her. Normal everyday Janes did not see ghosts. Perhaps the chemo had fried her brain a bit, or it had opened it up for new experiences. She took a long walk on her property and then spent the rest of the day putting the house into order. She could hardly wait until it was dark.

After supper, she read a book to put her to sleep and was not surprised to come awake just before 3:00.

She hurried downstairs and sat in her chair, waiting for the woman in white, concentrating only on seeing her. Then, as if it were quite natural, the woman was there again. This time, as she came into view, Kate saw she really wasn't wearing white. There was just a glow around her body. The image wavered and solidified. Five people sat around a table, their hands joined. She didn't recognize any of them from the photos she'd seen of the Smiths and Nelsons.

"Kate? Are you there?" the whisperer said. The woman looked up, her head moving as if in slow motion, the white glow shaking and then becoming still when she stopped.

They looked as though they were having a seance. Kate remembered holding seances on overnight camping trips when she'd been a Girl Scout. It had been an excuse to giggle and scream. These people looked quite serious. And they were calling her? It couldn't be. They were the ghosts; she was alive. It had to be another Kate. Hesitating, Kate got up from her chair and moved closer. "I can feel something," one of them whispered, the words floating through the house like a breeze through autumn-dried leaves. "Kate, if you're there, give us a sign," the dark-haired woman said. Kate giggled, a Girl Scout again.

"I am here," she said.

The woman nodded, as if she'd expected it all along.

"How are you, Kate Hein?" the woman asked.

Startled, Kate stopped walking around the circle.

"What? How?"

"Don't be frightened," the woman said.

"Ask her about Jenny. Have you seen my daughter Jenny? She's been dead three weeks," said another woman.

"Let me—" the dark-haired woman tried to interrupt.

"Can you tell us what it's like? Being dead?" a man asked.

Kate backed up and crashed into a table. Five heads turned toward her. "Look, there she is."

Someone screamed. The clock began chiming. The image faded away.

Kate breathed deeply, listening to her heart. The house's silence pounded her ears. Her cotton night shirt felt soft against her skin. Her mouth was dry. And she felt the floor firmly beneath her. She saw the moon outside. She had to be alive. She pinched her arm; it hurt.

What was happening? Had she died on the operating table and this was hell? No, it was too pleasant. Maybe heaven. This was what it was like to die and you never found out unless someone summoned you via a seance.

She ran to the phone and dialed her apartment.

"Jeff? It's Kate. Jeff, you've got to tell me. Did I die when I was operated on?"

"What?" he asked sleepily. "What are you talking about? Are you all right? Of course you didn't die."

"How do you know?" she asked, and then realized he wouldn't know if he was part of it all. This was crazy. Impossible. There had to be another reason.

"I'll leave now, Kate, and be there tomorrow night," he

said.

She didn't object. She told him to drive carefully and hung up the phone. Sitting in the kitchen, she listened to the birds come awake one by one.

She didn't want to work anymore. She had told Jeff that during the treatments.

"I want to live in the country and enjoy life," she said. "All I'll need is food, and I'll grow my own."

"Why can't we live in the country and work, too?" Jeff had asked.

"I didn't say we," she said. "I'm not going to make you live in the country. You'd hate it."

"How can you know that when I don't?"

One thing about her past she wouldn't change was Jeff. He had always been there when she needed him, always supportive. When she had gotten sick, she found herself moving away from him, half angry with him all the time.

Now she wished he would get there. She looked out the window again. It would be dark soon, and she didn't want to be alone, didn't want to think she was dead.

There had to be another explanation. She thought of the dark-haired ghost woman and her companions, trying to remember everything: Perhaps details would help her. The woman asking after Jennifer had worn a red smock that matched her bright red hair; the dark-haired woman had on jeans and a sweater; one man looked as if he had on a robe. She couldn't see their faces clearly enough to describe them. The table had a shiny surface, perhaps glass, reflecting the light of a single candle. Were they people from another part of the world, their thoughts linked with hers?

That did not explain why they thought she was dead.

Jeff's car rolled across the gravel driveway. Looking concerned, he got out of the car and ran toward the house. She opened the door, and they embraced. He smelled of Jeff, a warm musky smell that made her hold him tighter.

"I missed you," she said.

He pulled away and looked down at her.

"Are you all right?" he asked.

"Come on in. I'll tell you all about it."

She related her experiences while they sipped tea and ate brightly colored salad, losing some of her fear as she talked. Jeff took the story at face value, just as she knew he would.

"So you thought you were dead?"

She grimaced and then smiled. "I never overreact, do I?"

"Oh no," he said. "When you found out you were sick, you called to have your tombstone made the next day."

"Luckily I decided not to tempt fate," she said, laughing. "Let's come downstairs tonight and see if you can figure out what is going on. Are you up to it?"

"I'll go to sleep after I eat, and you can wake me when it's time."

Kate put Jeff to bed, tucking him in as if he were a child.

"I left some things in the car," he murmured before drifting off.

Kate put on the floodlight and went outside. Inside the car were all of their plants, three suitcases, and Lockheart, their cat, asleep on a pile of clothes. She opened her eyes, meowed and stretched. Kate shook her head and picked the cat up. She protested at first; she was fond of the car, but she soon realized Kate was warmer.

Kate had not wanted the cat or the plants, and she felt a twinge of anger as she unloaded the car. They all required responsibility. Plants needed water; cats had to be fed. And people got sick and died. Of course, Jeff could not have called neighbors up at 3:00 A.M. and asked them to cat and plant sit.

Once inside, Lockheart sniffed at her litter box and food and then padded upstairs to sleep with Jeff. Just like home, Kate thought.

When she grew tired, Kate went to bed, curling herself around Jeff and the cat. At 2:30, she shook Jeff awake. They shut the door behind them and went down to the living room where they sat in the dark until it was almost three. Kate began to wonder if it would happen at all; perhaps she had made it up. Then the woman shimmered into view.

"Kate Hein, come back to us. We didn't mean to frighten you," the woman said. The others joined her.

"Do you see them?" Kate whispered. She was relieved when Jeff nodded; she hadn't made it all up.

Kate stood and went to them. Tonight she could see more details: a counter behind the table, a beauty mark on the man's left cheek, a window—her window.

"Give us a sign," the woman said.

Reaching into the light, Kate picked up a cup from the counter. She couldn't feel it, but it moved and crashed to the floor. They all jumped.

Kate pulled her hand back. The clock chimed. She looked at Jeff, and the picture faded.

Jeff fumbled with the light and then sat down.

"Let me sit for a minute," he said.

Kate heard the cat crying upstairs. She went up and let her out.

"They looked different," Jeff said as she came down. "Didn't they? Their clothes. That room. It was like this one only a bit different."

"I know. The clothes weren't old-fashioned," Kate said. She smiled. "Not like I would have expected from ghosts."

"They did call to you," he said. "Maybe there's another Kate Hein somewhere."

"They're calling to her in this house? Doubtful," she said. "Why would they be in this room, in this house, calling me? Why do they think I'm dead? I'm not!"

"You will be someday in the future," he said, "in the far, far future."

"I'll be dead in the future. Yes, that's right," she said, suddenly excited. "I'm not dead now but I will be in the future, Jeff, so *they* could be from the future. Instead of holding a seance and getting the dead me, they get the past, with me in it."

"A kind of time travel?"

"I suppose," she answered, pacing the room. "Maybe in the future this house is haunted—strange noises in the night, things like that. Maybe I grow old and die here. They think I'm the one who is haunting the house, so they call me. To me the house is haunted, too, but it's haunted by the future! A window which goes both ways."

She laughed. "Think of it! Maybe many of the so-called haunted houses are really time windows—pieces of the future or past flickering back and forth with no one ever suspecting because both ends believe it's the nether regions."

"That's a better explanation than your first one," Jeff said.

Lockheart jumped onto Jeff's lap and he stroked her. "I wish there was one of these windows in the house I grew up in," Kate said, stopping to gaze across the yard.

Jeff sighed. "Why? So you could tell little Katie to eat right and move away from the dump? What would that have accomplished? Your parents would have taken you to a shrink and you would have grown up terrified of this woman who told you you would get cancer," Jeff said. "You can't change the past."

She walked across the room and dropped down on her knees in front of his chair. "But maybe I can change the future. Those people know who I am, for some reason; and in their time I'm dead. They could tell me why and how. I would know." She grabbed his hands. "I could stop being afraid. No more ifs."

"Katie," he said, cupping her face in his hands. "What does it matter? You can't live the future or the past. What if you find out I die in two years or you die a pauper or you win the Pulitzer or you live to be a hundred? Would you want to know any of those things ahead of time, really?"

She moved away from him.

"How can you understand? How can you sit there and pretend you do? You don't have a time bomb inside of you!"

"Is that why you've been so angry with me?" he asked. "Because I didn't get sick? Well, how do you know I don't have a 'time bomb' inside of me?" He started to leave the room. She reached for his arm.

"Don't you see? That's what I'm afraid of."

The house seemed even more warm and alive the next morning. Lockheart climbed along the counters while Jeff fixed breakfast.

"I tried the tractor again the other day," Kate said as they ate. "It still works. I wish it were spring so I could plant. All organic. I'll have complete control."

"I? Aren't you going to let me help?"

"It's something I want to do by myself," she answered. "Besides, I doubt you'll be here much of the time, will you? What would you do out here?"

"Eat what you grow," he said. "This is an interesting part of the state. We could do a back-to-nature book. I married you for better or worse. Don't the vows hold for both of us?"

"That's not nice," Kate said.

"I don't feel nice, Katie," he said. "I want to be with you, but only in the here and now, not with you angry about the past and worrying about the future."

Kate looked at her food and wished the night would come.

She moved slowly out of bed, trying not to disturb the cat or Jeff.

"Don't tell me," Jeff whispered. "Whatever you learn, I don't want to know."

She started to answer him, but instead she tiptoed out of the room and went downstairs. She sat in the chair waiting for her future and thinking about her past.

What she didn't like about the past was that she had no control of it. She had trusted the world to let her grow up unharmed, and it had failed her. Her doctor had told her she shouldn't blame her illness on any one thing: It was a combination of factors, nothing she could do about it now. She felt the anger ball in her. Nothing she could do now, but soon she would know her future and she would be prepared.

But would that give her more choices? Or would she just feel as if she were a puppet or actor playing out a role?

Was Jeff a part of her future? Jeff, the cat, and the plants the cat was always eating? She smiled. She liked the house better with them all in it.

The woman came into being in a milky glow, followed by the others.

"Are you there, Kate Hein?" the woman whispered.

"I'm here," Kate answered.

The people looked at each other and then warily about the room.

"Ask her," the other woman said.

"Kate, Mrs. Packard wants to know if you've had contact with her daughter Jennifer. Jenny passed away a short time ago."

Kate looked around the room. The plants made pointed silhouettes in the dark. Upstairs she heard Lockheart scratching at the door. Kate rubbed her stomach where she was still warm from Jeff's body pressed against hers as they slept.

"Tell Mrs. Packard that Jennifer is here with us, and she sends her love."

The clock struck three, and the window closed.

Up Above the World So High
Mario Milosevic

Anny sang wherever she wanted to. On deck, belowdecks, it didn't matter.

"Why do you sing?" I asked her once. She looked at me strangely.

"Why does anyone sing, Camille?"

"I don't know," I said.

So she took me to the topmost deck. Fifty feet or more above the waves, with the masts rising even higher, wavering and sliding against the pink sky. I looked at my feet to keep from getting dizzy.

"Now *listen*," she whispered.

The ship creaked. Chickens clucked and goats bleated from

the stern. Faint rumblings came from the decks below.

I didn't hear what she wanted me to hear. The ship: that was all I knew or cared about. But Anny knew something more. She was topside almost every chance she could get. She listened to the wind and the ocean; then she tried to imitate them with her songs.

I miss Anny a lot now. I even miss her songs that I never understood. That time on the deck, she tried so hard to show me. She made me close my eyes, made me concentrate on the water. Then she started humming. Very faintly at first, getting louder and louder, until she was as loud as the wind.

"Now do you see? The ocean is telling me something. It's telling us all something if only we'd listen."

I nodded. But she could see I was only trying to be nice.

"Do you realize there is a lot more to the world than this ship?" she asked.

"*World* is big. Without it we couldn't survive."

"*World* is a big boat, but just a boat. We can't live here forever, and someday we'll have to land. We've only lasted this long because many of us died in the first big storm and we were able to stretch our supplies for years."

"If we leave *World* we die," I said. "That's the truth."

I guess if you had to call Anny anything, it would have to be a dreamer. She got a job on mast and sail maintenance, once. It was dangerous work, but she was small and could scamper around the masts and get into tight places a lot easier than many others. I think that was where she learned so much about the ocean. "The boat is so tiny," she told me. "You can see it moving up and down on the water. At times I feel so

                                        MARIO MILOSEVIC

small. It's like this huge ocean is going to swallow up *World* and everyone on it."

She even stayed out during storms. I can still picture her hanging on to the sails, buffeted by the violent winds and rains and singing her songs. The first time she did that, she came to my room afterward. She was shivering and her long hair clung to her shoulders. "Do you have a blanket?"

"Anny! What have you done to yourself?"

She smiled. "Nothing."

I pulled her from the door and helped her out of her wet clothes.

Anny was a year older than me, but my fourteen-year-old body was much more developed than hers. She was so thin! "What's wrong with you?" I asked. "Are you sick?"

She covered herself with my blankets. "Nothing. I'm fine."

"Have you been eating?"

"You're not my mother. Leave me alone."

"I'm worried about you."

"Please, Camille. Will you get me something hot to drink?"

I made some tea for her. I had to use what was left of my week's ration, but I didn't mind. Anny was my friend.

"What were you doing?" I asked.

When she told me, I refused to believe her. My parents had told me about the storm that carried away all our small craft and killed a lot of people on board, including the captain and most of the crew.

"No one could survive that," I said. "You'd be blown off

the rigging."

"Nevertheless," she said, "that is what I was doing. You can believe me or not, I don't care."

Maybe she had a death wish. She certainly believed her life was not worthwhile aboard *World*. Only during a storm did she feel part of the world she wanted so terribly much. But it was a world she could never have. I told her so.

"Camille," she answered, "some people don't belong in the time and place where they are born. I should have been born when *World* was first setting out. Then we were full of the spirit of adventure. Now it's all gone, and we can never get it back. Sometimes that makes me so sad. You laugh at my songs—"

"No! I just—"

"Don't. I understand; I am a comical figure. You laugh at my songs, but sometimes my songs turn to tears, and if you heard me then you wouldn't laugh."

She wept, and I held her thin body close. I felt I could smother her if I held her too tight. "It'll be all right," I said. "After you're all warm and dry you'll feel much better." She sighed deeply, and I couldn't tell if it was from exasperation or contentment.

Harry, Anny's boss, soon found out she was climbing the masts at night and fired her. He didn't want any deaths on his crew, he said. It didn't stop her, though, and I even went with her once.

We waited until dark, when most of the ship was asleep. I slipped out of my room very quietly so as not to wake my

                                        MARIO MILOSEVIC

parents and met Anny two decks above, near the library.

I greeted her cheerfully, but she shushed me. We went up to the topmost deck, where the cold chilled us. I looked up. We were right beside the mainmast, but even on that clear night, with a full moon shining, the mast climbed much farther than my eye could follow. The sails hung limply from the yards. The night was still. Anny swung a length of rope.

"I swiped this from Harry," she said.

I nodded.

The lowest yard was more than twenty feet above us. Anny expertly threw her rope over it—there was a weight attached—and we used it to help us scamper up the mast, which was a good six or seven feet in diameter, almost impossible to climb any other way. I didn't know rope climbing, but Anny showed me how to use my feet, one over the other, with the rope between them and around my thigh. She was very patient with me.

When we reached the yard I rested, catching my breath while she pulled the rope up. The mainsail hung like a great weight below us. There was barely a ripple in it from top to bottom.

"Ready?"

Anny had already stood up, and was hanging on to the bottom of the topsail, which hung above us, even bigger than the mainsail. From the way she stood so confidently, I guessed she didn't need to hang on to anything. I loved *World*. It was my ship as much as it was Harry's, or my parents', or even Anny's. But there were some parts of it I preferred to just look at, not experience.

"I'm not sure, Anny. Maybe this isn't such a good idea."

"Don't be afraid. I'm here. I'll look after you."

I didn't want to admit to fear, so I agreed.

"Let's go," I said.

There were ratlines the rest of the way. I think it took us a good hour to get to the top, with Anny leading the way, constantly looking down to see how I was doing. We stopped for me to rest at each yard.

I didn't notice the swaying of the ship until we had passed the skysail and had crawled inside the crow's nest. Anny was hardly even breathing hard but I was sprawled on the deck unable to move. I could see her hair swaying very slowly, and it took me a minute to realize the motion was caused by the ship moving back and forth.

"We're moving, Anny! We're moving!"

"Of course we're moving. That's the rocking of the waves. It goes on all the time."

"But—"

"Down below you don't feel it so much because you are too close to the waves. But where we are now, the motion is amplified by the length of the mast. Up here you know you're on the ocean."

"I don't like it," I said. "I think I'm getting sick."

There was about six feet of mast extending past the crow's nest into the sky. I watched as it swung against the stars and my stomach followed the motion with a heavy sensation that wanted to crawl up my throat into my mouth.

"Don't look at the mast," said Anny. "That's what's making you sick."

"Uh-huh," I managed.

Now she started giggling. "Camille, close your eyes, dammit."

She put her hand over my face, and I felt better.

"Thank you," I said, feeling foolish. After a few seconds: "You can take your hand away now." She sat against the bulkhead, facing me.

"Yours is probably the first case of seasickness aboard the *World* in a very long time," she said, grinning.

"Hilarious."

"But never mind," she said, suddenly serious. "It's good to get that out of your system." I closed my eyes, feeling the sweat begin to evaporate from my body. I don't know how long I was there, lying peacefully, oblivious of the night around me. Eventually I became aware of Anny humming a song. It was one I'd heard her sing before. It went like this:

> *Twinkle, twinkle, little star,*
> *How I wonder what you are.*
> *Up above the world so high,*
> *Like a diamond in the sky.*

"Where did you hear that song?" I asked.

"My parents used to sing it to me."

"I like it."

She shrugged. "It's too simple. Listen to this one."

Then she started singing that weird stuff again. I couldn't understand a word. It wasn't English. It just wasn't *anything*. "Can't you sing something better?" I said.

"Do you want me to sing Twinkle-twinkle-little-star?"

"Well . . ."

"Let's look at the stars." She went to the rail and I joined her, being careful not to look down at the deck. Anny pointed out the North Star, and the Big Dipper, and Orion. She tried to show me Cassiopeia—"It's like a big 'W,' only bent a bit out of shape"—but I couldn't see it.

"Why do you like the ocean so much?" I asked.

"I don't. I hate it."

"But everything you do, the way you act—I don't understand."

"The ocean is my means of escape, nothing more."

"Where? Where can you escape to?"

"To land, Camille. That's where the future is. Not on this boat, this oversized piece of wood. It's dying. And everyone aboard it is dying."

I felt hurt. Suddenly we weren't close anymore. "I love *World*. It's my home."

"It's my home, too, but that doesn't mean it can't kill me. *World* was never meant to sail the ocean forever. When the ice caps started to melt, people were turning savage and there was less and less land all the time. People built ships to get away, but we were only supposed to sail for a little while, until the danger was over on the land."

I shook my head. "No. It can't be. We'd die without this ship."

"I'm building one of my own."

"Where, how?" I felt ill again.

"I have a secret place. It's not a boat really, just a raft. But it's a good one. I steal wood from the carpentry shop and canvas from the sailmakers. I've been saving my food. I even have enough rope to lower my raft into the water when the time comes. There. I've told you everything." She looked so vulnerable that I wanted to squeeze her tight. "There's enough room and food for two people, Camille. Will you come with me?"

Her desperation only made me pity her more. "Why? Why should I? Why should you? What could you accomplish?"

What happened next I didn't understand. She started getting ready to leave. I kept asking her my question over and over, trying to get her to answer. She ignored me, pulled up the hatch and began climbing down. I followed as quickly as I could, not wanting to be left alone so high up.

But when we got to the mainsail yard she stopped. I struggled to climb beside her. "What are you waiting for?"

"We're going to go down a different way," she said.

"What way? What are you talking about?"

"When *World* first set sail the kids had a game. They would climb up here on calm days, and slide down the mainsail. It was great fun."

"How do you know what happened years ago?"

"I've read the logs. So should you. Then you'd know I'm telling you the truth about *World*. Now how about it, are you going to slide down with me?"

I tried to study her face by the moonlight, but it was in shadow. I looked at the sail past my feet. The deck was a long way down. "Have you ever done it?"

"Lots of times."

The tone in her voice told me she was lying. It wasn't that she was scared, it was like she was defying me to disbelieve her.

"What if it breaks, or tears or something?"

"It won't."

"What if a wind comes up and billows out the sail?"

"The air is calm and you know it."

"I don't know, Anny. It's a long way down, what's going to break our fall?" My palms were getting sweaty. I was sure she could feel me shivering.

"Our weight will stretch the sail so it'll make a trampoline at the bottom. The friction of our bodies against it will slow us down."

"I don't believe you. You're making all this up."

"Listen to me, Camille. You know I'm telling the truth. They really did this. They did it all the time."

"No. I won't do it. It's crazy."

She grabbed me. I jumped back, but she was too strong for me. Such a thin body, but what power! It startled me, and then it was too late.

"Hang on!" she shouted. I felt a shove and grabbed at her as I lost my balance.

That was the last thing we did together. While we were making all that noise, someone heard us and called for Harry to find out what was going on. Furious, he waited at the bottom and yelled at us that we could have killed ourselves. I was too dazed to worry about him, though. Anny just smiled.

My parents confined me to quarters for two weeks, and I

                                    MARIO MILOSEVIC

couldn't see Anny. I didn't lose contact with her, though. She managed to get a letter to me disguised as a note from someone else. This is what it said:

Dear Camille:

They say I've created a nuisance and will try me as a grown-up. I can't let them do that because they might find out about my raft and take it away from me. So I have to leave the ship soon. Tomorrow or the next day.

I am doing what's right. On land we can find the other ships. Spaceships they are called. The bold and the brave went on those ships to look for a better planet. We must find land. From land we can get to space. You know where I am. I want you to come with me. Please, Camille, join me.

ANNY

There was a line of little words like "dum" and "dee" at the bottom of the page that I didn't understand.

I read the letter once quickly, then put it away—and kept taking it out every few minutes. Anny was a misfit aboard the *World*. I decided we would be better off without her. We had tried to be friends, but we were too different.

When I came to that realization, a great peacefulness fell over me. It was the same feeling as when you've cleaned up your room and everything is neat and in its place. You can rest with a clear mind. That's what I did. I fell asleep.

Anny was reported missing the next day. My parents told me about it. She had escaped from her room, probably through the ventilation shaft. Anny could squeeze through almost any hole. They searched for her for days. I knew they would never find her.

When my two weeks were up, I explored the whole ship all over again, I was so happy to be free. I could tell, somehow, that Anny wasn't on board anymore. I cried a little, once, but only a little because I knew she was where she wanted to be.

My parents were trying to get me interested in a guy they liked a lot. He lived a couple of decks below us but I thought he was boring. I didn't see him very much. Mostly I concentrated on school.

Although *World* is a big ship, it is so crowded that people tend to stay to themselves to get as much privacy as possible. I know very little about the people who live next door even. It wasn't until I started reading the ship's logs that I found out who the original captain was. Captain Tyler her name was. Or his name. It didn't say if Tyler was a man or a woman and no one I knew could tell me. Not the librarian, not my parents, not my friends. It was then that I realized how small *World* really was, how big we tried to make it by pushing away other people, making them into strangers. I felt like I needed Anny again, only this time she wasn't with me and I would never see her again.

About three months after the incident in the crow's nest, we began to sight land more and more often. No one could explain it and nobody but me seemed to be excited about it. I suppose I wondered if Anny had managed to get to one of those distant lines on the horizon. When I looked at them, I thought I could hear her songs again, clear as a cloudless sky. I begged my parents to let me go ashore. They said it was too dangerous because of wild animals and primitive people, and besides, the ship couldn't get close enough anyway.

I knew they were only scared. So was everyone else. I sat in my room and read Anny's letter. I noticed the last line again, and this time something clicked. I read the words slowly and remembered Anny humming her tune when we were in the crow's nest. Not the "Twinkle, twinkle" song but the other one that I didn't like. That song and the line in the letter were the same. The sounds were like a longing cry, a wail of despair. I closed my eyes and remembered Anny singing it.

I wanted a closer look at the shores we were passing, and I knew there was only one place for that. The next morning I climbed up to the crow's nest. I wore white clothes and shoes and even a white hat so that no one would notice me in the daylight.

I thought the thing I found in the crow's nest was only a pile of rags at first, but as I pulled myself in, one end of the pile raised itself and Anny's face, shrunken and thin, peered at me with squinting eyes.

She was even more thin than I remembered her, but she sat up and greeted me. "I was wondering how long it would take you to find me here," she said. Her voice was weak.

"I wasn't looking for you. I thought you were gone months ago."

She nodded. "Of course. That's what I wanted everyone to think."

"Even me?"

"Well . . . I wasn't sure about you. I didn't know whose side you were on. On the night that I wanted to go, I came to your quarters and I saw you."

"I don't remember—"

"You were asleep. But I could see that you hadn't got any-thing ready for our trip. You were glad to be rid of me, weren't you?"

I didn't answer.

"Anyway, I decided that was it. There was just nothing at all for me here anymore. And I went to get my raft."

"But you lost your nerve before you could do it, right?"

She laughed. The sound was dry and rasping, like an old woman's laugh. It made me flinch.

"Hardly," she said. "What happened was—what happened, was that I made the raft too big to get out. I built it in this deserted little closet room that was just big enough for me and the raft, but the door was real tiny, and, well, I just didn't allow for it." She laughed again, shaking her head. "A year's work, completely wasted. The doorframe was metal. Metal! Steel, I think. I just sat there, stunned. It would have taken a month or more to take the thing apart and find another hiding place to put it back together again."

My face was calm, but inside I was screaming. Anny had never really wanted to leave. She was as tied to this ship as any of us! Her grand dream was just a dream that she was too frightened to make real. I hated her and I hated my romanti-cization of her.

"What did you do?"

"I climbed up here. It was the only place I had to think things over."

"And?"

"I decided I'd been doing it all wrong. I was building a boat while I was on board a ship. That was stupid. So I've been steering the *World* myself. At night, when the automatic pilot is on, I sneak in and change the heading. The people that run this ship are dim anyway—they don't know where they're going or how to get there."

I was going to tell her how crazy she was, but she interrupted me.

"Camille, dear, there's no reason for you to not go with me. Do you see that now? Already I've brought us within sight of land many times, you must have noticed. Eventually I'll bring us close enough so we can swim ashore. Or we don't even have to swim, we can just float. You'll see, we can do it."

I looked at her shrunken body. She couldn't possibly have swum the width of *World,* let alone the miles to shore.

Why is it that things always seem better in your memory? I had thought Anny was my hero. Now that I saw her again, she was a nothing.

I couldn't stand to be with her anymore. I said, "Stay here, Anny. I'll be right back with some food. We'll get through this together. Okay?"

Her head had been tilted forward, anticipating and prompting my response, which, when it came, made her relax abruptly. "Thank you," she whispered.

When I reached the deck again I called Harry and told him where he could find Anny. I warned him to be careful with her or I'd kill him in his sleep. He laughed, but he knew I was serious.

I'm not ashamed of what I did. The only person I ever

knew who wasn't satisfied with life aboard *World* turned into an emaciated animal. She sang songs, but she didn't eat. She wasn't sensible, and that's what you have to be.

I still have Anny's letter and I still read that last line whenever I start to get nostalgic about the stars. It makes me laugh, now, to think of those poor souls that left this planet to go to space.

Harry was careful with Anny, and I took care of her for a while until she died. She was too weak to go on. Poor Anny had wasted all her strength on a vision that could never come true.

Sanctuary
Kim Antieau

I went back to the house yesterday. At first it seemed too different. The long twisting drive was almost overgrown. The lawn was covered with weeds; Kiri's flowers had all since died. Then I looked up at the pine trees swaying in the wind and heard the gentle noise of the sea air winding through them. My chest tightened and the memories came rushing back. I wondered, as I have wondered nearly every hour of my life for five years, how I could have done what I did to Kiri.

In the summer before my last year of college, I came to the tiny coastal town of Canyons to work in my uncle's store. I accepted his offer of work because I wanted to experience small town life. I had spent most of my life in cities and, as a future psychologist, I thought I should learn to deal with all kinds of people. And I needed a job.

My uncle's store served as a food, drug, and feed outlet for the town. Everyone knew my uncle Bob and within the week everyone knew me. First suspicions appeared to be instantly allayed when people were told: "This is Bob's nephew Jason." For the first week it seemed my entire name was "Bobsneph-ewjason."

Since I served as delivery person as well as stocker and cashier, I was able to see most of the town and some portions of the beach within the first week. I began to learn what home belonged to which people. Most of the houses were single-story frames, bent and crooked, as if shaped by the constant sea wind.

There was one house, however, that stood out among the others. I spotted it on a delivery run one afternoon. I stopped the car and looked up the drive. The house was built on a hill overlooking the beach and town. Tall evergreens shielded the wooden and stone two-story building from the winds. To one side of it was an enclosed greenhouse, and when I squinted, I could just make out a figure inside, bending over. Someone honked behind me, and I started up the car and left. Later I asked my uncle about it.

"That's the Marlin home. Kiri Marlin lives there."

"All by herself?"

"Yep," he answered, heaving a box of juice off the shelf and onto the dolly. I grabbed another and stacked it on top.

"Have I ever seen her in here?"

"No," he answered. "She doesn't leave her house."

"What?" I had visions of discovering a truly remarkable psychological case. I could study her, do a paper about her. I would become famous before graduating.

"I'd like to meet her," I said. "Does she see people?"

My uncle stopped bending and looked over at me. "Of course she sees people. I deliver her groceries once a week. She's just a lady who doesn't leave her house. Her parents were sort of eccentric, too."

"Actually, it isn't eccentricity. It's a condition called agoraphobia. It literally means an abnormal fear of open places. I didn't know it could run in families."

"She's not afraid of open places, Jason. She just doesn't leave her house. She used to, but she hasn't since her parents died."

"Why? How did they die?"

"They just died."

"Could I deliver the groceries next time she calls?" I asked.

He reluctantly agreed. "I'm only allowing this because you are a relative, not really an outsider. I'm trusting you not to bug her. We all like Kiri. She's part of this town and we don't want anything to happen to her."

"I'm not going to hurt her," I said. "I'm nice to old ladies."

Bob smiled. "Quit talking and get to work."

Two days later, Kiri Marlin called in her order. I helped get the requested items together and then I anxiously drove to her house. When I got out of the car, I noticed there wasn't any wind. I could hear it in the pine trees, a gentle whooshing sound I liked to listen to on nights just before a storm, but I could not feel it like I could in town—a damp wind that never seemed to stop. It was peaceful here, as if I had stepped into some kind of haven. I listened for a moment before reaching into the car for the groceries.

I rang the doorbell and a voice called for me to come in. I was mildly surprised that the door was not locked. I opened it and went inside. I expected cobwebs, darkness, perhaps a stale wedding cake or an old woman in a dingy wedding gown. Instead I was greeted by two cats, sunlight, bleached oak floors, vivid green ferns, and various hanging plants. The air was cool and fresh, as if a breeze were running through the house.

And then Kiri walked into the room, a totally different apparition from the one I had expected. She removed gardening gloves and held out her hand. I was struck dumb, but I managed to shake her hand.

"You must be Jason," she said, tucking the gloves into her jean pockets. "I'm Kiri Marlin." She smiled, and I guessed her age at around thirty. Light brown hair was pulled away from her face by two combs. Her pretty cheeks were flushed, as if she had been outside running.

She laughed. "Close your mouth, Jason. Emily Dickinson I'm not. Come on into the kitchen," she said, taking one of the bags from me.

I blushed and followed her into a large airy kitchen, where windows and plants outnumbered appliances and cupboards.

One of her cats, a Siamese, leapt onto the counter and sniffed at the packages as I set them down.

"Are you enjoying your visit?" she asked as she began putting away the groceries.

"It's very different from where I come from," I answered.

"That doesn't answer my question," she said, "though I suppose it does in a way."

"Oh, I like it here, really, especially the ocean and the beaches."

"I like the ocean, too. Sunsets from here are spectacular," she said.

"You can see it from here?"

"Sure, I have quite a view," she said. "Come on, I'll show you."

She took me out of the kitchen and up a short flight of stairs into the living room. All of the west wall was made of glass. We were above the trees and had a panoramic view of the ocean. Today the water was dark green, flecked with white. A flock of birds flew over one of the shore rocks.

"It's nice, isn't it?" she said, smiling.

I nodded and turned from the window. I suddenly felt guilty for my earlier desire to examine her like some kind of specimen.

"Do you like games?" I asked, noticing several boxes on her bookshelves: a backgammon game, a go set, Scrabble.

"Yes, I guess I do."

"I've always wanted to learn go. Could you teach me?"

She turned and looked into my eyes for several seconds, as if she were trying to look deeper, to see into my soul.

"Sure, I'll teach you," she said. "You bring the pizza and be here at eight."

Kiri was a good and gentle teacher, but when I did something totally wrong, she reprimanded me, telling me I had not been listening. After nearly an hour in her company, I forgot she had this little quirk: She did not leave her house. We played and ate in the living room so we could watch the sun go down. As the evening passed, she asked me about school and my life, and I told her. She teased me when I told stories about parties I had attended in college.

"I don't want to hear about that," she said. "I want to know what you've learned. Not just at school, but in your lifetime."

"I'm not sure what I've learned," I said, "except how little I truly know." I was surprised at the things I could tell her— feelings and ideas I wasn't even aware of until I said them to her.

The cats each chose a lap and curled up to sleep.

"I've had Harlow, the Siamese, since my mother died," she said. She leaned against the couch and stroked the cat.

"When was that?" I asked.

"About eight years ago," she answered. "She's getting to be an old cat. I got Tori three years ago."

"How did your mother die?" I asked.

"Just like most people die," she answered. "She stopped living."

I remembered that my uncle hadn't told me how her parents had died, and I wondered what the big mystery was. I didn't pursue it, however, and the conversation moved away from her mother. We discussed books we had each read. I will remember that first evening always. Sometimes, now, I wish I could forget, or at least distort it so I don't remember how beautiful it was. That night, as always with Kiri, I was relaxed. There was no flirtation, no awkwardness between us. I just truly enjoyed the company of another person. The house creaked, the pines moved with the wind, and Kiri and I talked into the night.

Finally, when night was edging toward morning, I told Kiri I should leave. We cleaned the living room and then she walked me to the door. I hesitated, not wanting to go.

"May I come again?" I asked.

She looked into my eyes.

"You must know one thing, Jason," she said. "I do not leave this house. You must promise not to try to change that."

"I promise," I said, without thinking. She smiled. I would have promised anything that night just so I could see her again.

For the next week, I went over to Kiri's every night. Sometimes there were other people there, friends of hers. Some of them were people I had met in town or had seen roaming the beaches. They were nice, but I resented their presence. I wanted Kiri all to myself. She seemed to enjoy our time alone, too, showing me how she managed without leaving the house.

She was obviously proud of her greenhouse. It was filled with flowers and vegetables. I had never seen flowers so colorful or vegetables so lush, yet she used no fertilizers or other chemicals.

"Just my hands," she said.

I was not much of a gardener, but since Kiri enjoyed spending time in the greenhouse, I asked her to teach me how to be useful.

"I think teaching you to be useful would be a full-time job," she said, grinning.

I grabbed her. "I'll get you for that," I said. "I'll yell at your plants and give them neuroses."

She laughed, and I realized she was in my arms. My stomach seemed to twist inside itself. It still does when I think of that moment. I had never felt anything so wonderful—until I leaned over and kissed her. She put her arms around me, and we embraced.

She whispered my name and kissed me again.

"We're all dirty from the garden," she said. "I think we need a shower." She took my hand and we went upstairs.

I had never fallen so quickly and so much in love. We never ran out of things to say, yet often we just lay quietly in each other's arms, listening to the wind through the pines. One evening, we fell asleep on the couch together. I awakened to darkness; Kiri was gone. When my eyes adjusted to the dark, I could see Kiri by the window. I went and stood behind her. The moon was out, shining down on the beach and ocean. Two people walked along the tide mark. I put my arms around Kiri's waist.

"Do you wish you were down there?" I whispered.

"Good God, no," she answered, stiffening in my arms. "If all around you were flames and you were in the only safe spot, would you want to go into the flames?"

"Is that what it's like for you?" I asked. "Is it that frightening?"

"It is not so much frightening as . . ." She turned to me, searching for the right words. "As certain. I will die if I leave this house."

"But you will die inside this house someday, too," I said. "Think of all the things we could do together, places we could see before we die."

She covered my mouth with her hand. "Ssssh. You promised. You must accept me the way I am."

"Won't you even consider going for help?"

"Help? I don't need help, Jason." She pulled away from me.

I took her hand. "Can't you see it's not normal to be locked up in this house?"

She laughed, making it an almost unnatural sound. "Of course it's not normal. But it isn't just my psyche that's in danger, Jason. It's all of me." She sighed. "I've been out, and I'm nothing out there—insubstantial. Here, I'm something. I have control. Some people never find their niche in the world, I have. My parents tried to live outside this house. They failed. This is our spot. This is where I belong. I've accepted that. There is comfort in knowing where you belong, Jason.

"Kiri, I can help you if you let me," I said, as I took her face in my hands. "There is nothing outside this house that can't hurt you inside this house, too."

She stared at me, an unwavering look that made me think she was looking clear to my core. I dropped my hands.

"You can't understand," she said, "but you must accept that this is my place on Earth. End of discussion."

The conversation ended, but I continued to think about it. I needed to finish college. I couldn't do that in Canyons, but I didn't want to leave Kiri. I had always imagined myself traveling one day. I couldn't do that with Kiri, and I didn't want to go without her. I was so blind; if only I had realized how many places we saw together in her own home.

I was determined to cure her. I went to the library and found out what I could about agoraphobia. There wasn't much. They described physical reactions: perspiration, accelerated heartbeat, severe anxiety attacks. Therapists suggested gradually curing patients by taking them on small excursions outside the home.

One night I began looking through my uncle's library, hoping to find something to help me.

"Whatcha looking for, son?" Uncle Bob asked as he stood in the doorway.

"Psychology books."

He laughed. "Nothing but Zane Grey and Janet Dailey in this house," he said.

I smiled. I had never known anyone as well read as my uncle. The house was packed with books. Bob came into the room and sat down.

"Let it be, Jason. What does it matter?"

"I want to do things with her," I said. "It hurts me to see her holed up in that house all the time."

"Why? Is she unhappy?"

"She says she isn't. But how could she be happy? It must

feel like a prison."

"Or a sanctuary," he said. He leaned back in his chair. "She knows what's best for her, Jason. Her folks have been in this town, in that house, for generations. Made their fortune in the stock market, I believe. Before they died, Kiri's parents were important people in town." He squinted. "You know, I can hardly remember them anymore. It hasn't been that long since they died."

"How did they die?"

"Mr. Marlin was in a car accident," he said. "There were rumors he died before the car actually crashed into the ocean. There wasn't much left of him when they pulled the car out. It was the first time in decades he'd left the house. No one knew why he left. Some said Kiri's mother talked him into it." He shrugged. "Maybe it was a nice day and he wanted to go for a ride. Soon after his death, Kiri's mother walked into the ocean and drowned."

"So you think Kiri's fear comes from what happened to her parents when they left the house?"

"You aren't listening," he said. "Maybe she's got reasons to fear."

I shook my head. "There must be a way to help her, to free her from this fear. There must be."

Bob stood and stretched. "She doesn't have a problem with it, Jason. You do." He started to say something else, but instead, he left the room. I sat on the floor, wondering what to do next.

For weeks I worried about the end of the summer and the

rest of our lives. Then suddenly I had the answer and I was elated—and afraid. Kiri never suspected what I was going to do—at least I thought so at the time. I chose a day that was particularly cool and breezy. The air moved nicely through the house, filling it with the smells of the outdoors. Clouds covered the sun, taking the summer brightness away. Kiri and I worked in the greenhouse. I helped her take flowers and put them in the wheelbarrow. Later I was going to plant them outside, around the living room windows.

"I get enough sunlight from the windows, but sometimes I think my flowers need to be outside," she said. Harlow bounded into the room like a kitten and jumped onto my shoulders. Tori pawed at my leg and meowed.

"They're hussies, aren't they?"

"Just like you," I said. I reached over and kissed her nose.

"How did you get off work today?" she asked.

"I asked for it off."

"That was clever," she said, laughing. Then she scowled when I tugged too hard on a root and it broke. "Patience, Jay. In any case, I'm glad you're here. I love these kinds of days." She whirled around. "I can't believe how happy I am!"

I caught her in mid-turn. The cat jumped away from me. "Happy! Well, I've got something that will make you even happier. Close your eyes."

"What?" She closed her eyes. "A surprise?"

"Yes." I tied a kerchief around her eyes and across her ears. Then I twirled her around a few times. I led her around the house, going up and down stairs, trying to disorient her. We both laughed. My heart began pounding too hard. I broke out in a sweat. I hoped I was doing the right thing, but I was afraid she would be angry with me. I stopped her for a moment and kissed her. She lifted her head up, blind, and grinned.

"I love you very much," I told her, suddenly frightened of what I was doing.

"I love you, too," she said. "Now take me to my surprise."

I twirled her one more time, led her in and out of two more rooms, and then I took her through the open front door. I talked and laughed so she wouldn't notice the change. I had even put some old boards on the sidewalk, hoping they would feel like her living room floor. I stopped her just out of the shadow of the house, about ten steps from the door.

"Jason, where am I? Can I see now?"

I slowly untied the kerchief. "See, you're safe," I said.

I will never forget the look on her face as she turned to me. It still troubles me at night: I open my eyes from a nightmare and I will see her face, inches from my own. Her eyes were opened wide in terror—and disappointment. I had betrayed her.

"You promised," she whispered.

Suddenly, it seemed that the sky was black. Or was it? I couldn't breathe or move. Perspiration rolled down my back. I became overwhelmed with anxiety. I was dizzy. I covered my eyes, trying to still the twirling world. What was happening to me? I reached for Kiri, but my arms flayed air.

Seconds later, I opened my eyes. The dizziness subsided. I looked around. It was a gorgeous summer day. The cats stood in the doorway watching me. A breeze moved through the pine trees.

And Kiri was gone.

I ran toward the house, calling her name. Inside, I wandered about almost blindly, bumping into doors and walls: I knew when I found her she would not ever want to see me again.

But I didn't find her. She wasn't in the house. I looked around the yard, too, but there was nothing.

And then I went to the greenhouse and found something near the windows. I'm not certain what—it looked as if some living thing had suddenly become unglued and melted into the ground, leaving behind its shadow like a kind of marker. I closed my eyes and quickly backed away.

They never found Kiri. For a time I was suspected of murdering her. The more I went over the events in my mind, the more I believed that to be true, but when I confessed, they didn't believe me.

Soon after, Kiri's recently made will was read. She declared that her substantial fortune and the house be left to me if she was not seen in the house for thirty days. When my uncle told me, I cried out, calling for someone to take away the pain. I realized then she had known all along I would not keep my promise.

The house stood empty until my return yesterday. The cats had fled long ago. I stood at the door trembling. I turned the handle. It was unlocked, as it had always been. I wanted to be sick as I opened the door. It all came rushing back, every second of the happiness we had shared in this house. And then I stepped inside. This time I found the cobwebs and darkness

I had expected that first day. The house smelled of decay. I breathed the damp air deeply. I had done this. I was the cause. I looked around. The house was empty, as if Kiri had never existed.

I started to back away, to run out of the house, but something made me hesitate. Perhaps I could fix it up, make it alive again. I had traveled for five years, running toward anything that could make the memories go away even for a little while. Now I was weary of it. This was my home, my place in the world. I looked outside once more, and then I closed the door and shut away the light.

Winding Broomcorn
Mario Milosevic

Had a good crop of broomcorn this year. I harvested great sheaves of it and brought it into my shed. My wife Belle used to love to see it, stiff stalks, all different colors, rust and green and gold. Bundled up like dry rainbows is the way she used to put it.

Would sit with me then, watch me make my brooms. She especially liked the stitching I did at the end, where I bind the stalks together with thread almost as thick as string. She used to say there was nothing more attractive than a man doing something domestic like sewing.

Those days are gone. Now, she'd just as soon I got rid of the winding machine and spend all my time with her, but you know, husbands have to have something to do their wives don't understand.

I saw it a million times when I was marrying couples. The men always wanted hobbies. The women, well, the men *were* their hobbies. Not saying anything right or wrong about it. Just what it is.

My pastoring days are over now. Used to have a congregation over at Mill Town on the river. Can't say I miss it. For one thing, it takes a lot of your time. Belle used to hate it when I had to go to evening meetings at the church. Always something: AA meeting, bible study, bake sale planning, building up the food bank, getting the next rummage sale going. And on and on.

For another thing, there's a lot of pain involved with pastoring. People in trouble. Their kids sick or dying, or their spouses fooling around or addicted to drugs or the drink or gambling. All kinds of terrible stuff. People miserable for one reason or another and they came to me for help. For divine counsel.

I tried, but I don't know how much I did for them. Sometimes I wonder if I did any good at all. Only God can really help. Either you believe and get comfort or you don't and I never knew how to make people believe. Didn't know if it was right to even try.

Belle never came to my church. Belle isn't a believer. Says she needs evidence, but never seen any. Preferred sitting in the sun. Well, that's okay. Everyone is different. Made it awkward for me, though: a pastor who couldn't convince his own wife about God. What good could he be?

I sometimes wondered that myself.

Now we're a hundred miles away here in Grangeville in eastern Oregon. Lots of wheat farming and cows. Quiet. I grow my broomcorn and make brooms by hand, like my grandfather and mother did. A lost art now. Only old coots like me doing it and not too many of us, either.

But everyone needs a broom. I used to sell them, back in the day. Now I don't need the money so I give them away for wedding gifts. Or when people come to visit I give them a broom. People in town are always asking me for brooms to give to their friends.

Today I wanted Belle to come out to the shed. Watch me making brooms like she used to. That would be nice.

I looked around. Well, maybe this old shed wasn't clean enough for her.

I took one of my brooms and began sweeping the dust out from corners. I poked up into the crevices in the ceiling, brought down tangles of cobwebs. Brushed the walls with my broom, pulling away dust and pieces of dirt. I guess I had let it go just a little bit out here in the shed. Kind of grimy. Good to clean it all up. That's what a broom is for, right? I make them, why not use one of them?

I made a big pile of dust in the middle of the shed. I bent down with a dustpan. I was thinking about going and getting Belle to come sit with me when a woman walked into the shed. I stood up. Can't say how old she was. One of those people you think could be thirty or she could be sixty or anything in-between. She carried a walking stick bent every which way.

"Hello," she called as she stepped into the shed. "I hear

you wind brooms."

"That's right," I said. I put out my hand. "The name's Dwayne."

She leaned her stick against the wall, then touched my palm. I hardly felt anything, like she was made of air. "Pleased to meet you. I'm Kate."

"Hi, Kate."

"I was in Mill Town," she said, "and a woman named Alice said you were out here making brooms."

"I haven't seen Alice in ages. She and Belle were good friends. Where you from?"

"I'm from a lot of places," said Kate. "Passing through. Wanted to find out about the guy who makes brooms the old way."

"Yeah. I'm famous around here. People call me the broom whisperer." I laughed at my own dumb joke.

She smiled, went over to the stash of broomcorn and ran her hand over the bristles, like she was fascinated by them. "You been doing this long?" she said.

"My family's been making brooms for close on ninety years. This equipment was my granddad's. You interested in brooms?"

"I had one. A good one. But it broke."

"You mean the handle?" I said.

"Yes," she said. "The handle. And more than the handle. It wouldn't do what it was supposed to do anymore."

"Oh," I said. "Do you see any here you like?"

She studied the wall where I had several of my brooms hanging. They made a nice display.

"Those are impressive brooms," she said, "but I was wondering if you would make one special for me."

"Oh sure," I said. "If I can."

She handed me her walking stick. "Can you make a broom using this as a handle?"

The stick still had most of its bark on. It was anything but straight. It looked like a lightning bolt, zigging this way and zagging that.

"Sure," I said. "I can wind some broomcorn on that."

She pulled up a stool from a corner of the shed and sat down. "That's wonderful," she said. "Can you do it now?"

I've been making brooms a long time. Since I was nine years old, so that's almost seventy years, but no one has ever wanted a broom right *now*.

I laughed. "You sure need this broom, don't you?"

"I need it for my work."

"What work is that?" I asked.

"It's spiritual. I help people."

"Huh," I said. Noncommittal like. I wasn't exactly sure I wanted to tell her I used to be in the same business.

I took the stick from her and brushed off some of the looser bits of bark. I tried bending it, testing its strength. No go. It was a good solid piece of wood.

"It'll do, right?" she said.

"Yeah," I said. "It'll do fine."

I clamped it in the gripping jaw of the broom machine, then hammered a small nail on the end. I pulled out a bit of wire from the winder and twisted it around the nail. When it was good and secure, I went to the stash of broomcorn and pulled up a good big sheaf of it. I shook it to get rid of the seeds. They fell like bits of colored rain: red, green, and yellow drops. Clung to my shoes and pants. I placed some of the broomcorn around the end of the stick and sat down and started unwinding the wire with the foot pedal. I eased the wire around the bristles of broomcorn and added more bristles as the winding progressed. I started getting warm. Sweat popped up on my forehead.

"It's quite a process," said Kate.

"Uh huh," I said.

"Belle ever come in here and watch you make brooms?"

That sounded like a strange question.

"Not for a long time," I said. "She used to like it."

She nodded. "Yes, but how long?"

"Don't know exactly. Couple three years, I guess."

"Not since she died, right?"

The wire had the stalks wrapped pretty tight by this time. The thing already looked something like a real broom. All I had to do now was bend the bristles over the spooled wire and stitch up the broom so the bristles held together. That last part, the stitching, was what Belle really liked.

Kate didn't say anything else. Watched me. I heard her breathing.

"How'd you know about Belle?" I said.

"Call it a sixth sense. Or maybe a seventh or eighth. I lost count some time ago."

"Who are you?"

"Someone who needs a new broom. That's all."

I slipped on the leather mitt I used to help me push the

needle through the bristles. The mitt belonged to my mother a long time ago, from when she used to stitch brooms. I did a few stitches in silence, bent over, with the heat starting to get to me.

"You like to go around the countryside harassing widowers?" I said.

"It wasn't anything personal. I just noticed. Had to say something."

"Uh huh."

"It's mostly I couldn't help myself. You seem like you're in pain."

"Okay."

"I really do need the broom."

I kept stitching the bristles, making sure they were gathered up good and tight. Nothing worse than a broom that doesn't hold together to get at the dust hiding in cracks and crevices. You want that good strong sweeping action, or else what's the point? When I finished, I loosened the clamp and took the broom out. Held it out for her inspection. I didn't want to look in her eyes.

She took it and held the bristles up close, examining them.

"I usually trim the ends," I said. "At an angle for better sweeping, but I'm guessing you want it all raggedy like it is."

"Quite right," she said. "Good guess." She stood up and placed the unbristled end on the floor, like it was still a walking stick. She held it just at the base of where the bent bristles make a knob.

"What do I owe you?"

"Nothing. I make them for fun now."

She nodded. "Thank you."

I waved my hand.

"Some of us are gathering for a ceremony," she said. "To-night. You're welcome to come if you want."

"Oh, I've had lots of ceremonies in my life."

"One more won't hurt you."

"Probably won't help, either," I said.

"I'd really like you to come. We'll be up on the hill behind the firehouse at dusk. Thanks again for the broom."

She turned around and walked out of the shed.

Later I thought I should have said more to Kate about Belle. Explained how things were. Some people have that effect. You just want to *tell* them things and you don't know why. And then later you wonder why you didn't.

People in town knew I was married once, and a lot of people even knew Belle's name, but she died only a few months after we came to Grangeville, so not too many people here really *knew* her. Except me.

But the worst of it? I don't even go to church anymore. Me, who used to be a pastor, I can't understand God anymore, taking away Belle like that. When I was pastoring and people came to me with their grief, I used to tell them it was God's will. None of us could understand. We just had to have faith.

Well, I was only half right. I don't understand, but I also don't have faith anymore.

So I pretend Belle is still alive. In my mind, that's all. No one else has to know. No one else does know.

Until Kate.

After Kate left I made some more brooms until I got tired of making brooms. Then I went into the house and opened a can of soup and ate it while I watched Belle's favorite show, the one with the detective who sees crimes before they happen. I never much liked it, but it makes me think of Belle and I like anything that reminds me of her. I thought about that hill behind the firehouse. Who would have a ceremony there? In this town? Crazy.

The firehouse is only a block from my house. I can see the hill from my front window. I turned off the TV, got up from the couch, opened the front door, and stood at the screen door. The night was still warm, but a cool breeze was beginning to catch on the air. I heard noises coming from over beyond the firehouse: howls, hollering.

I saw an orange glow up near the top, too. Looked like a campfire. Some figures dancing around. Four or five. I couldn't tell exactly how many.

There's a thing that happens to people in grief. I saw it when I was at my old church: They dream about the person passed on, and they want to go live in that dream because it's the world they remember.

I knew that was what happened to me.

I also knew it wasn't good for me to be in that place for too long. A while, maybe, but if it drags on for months, well, that's a whole different story. And Belle's been passed on for years now.

Standing there at the door, the living room behind my back, I felt her. Belle. I thought if I turned around, then I would see her, sitting on the couch, watching her program.

I wanted to turn around.

Wanted to see her again. But I knew she wouldn't be there. Hadn't been there for a long time.

But the dancers around the fire. I heard their throaty calls to the darkness.

I pushed the screen door open.

It slammed shut behind me.

My shoes crunched on the gravel.

I didn't look back.

Not once.

I wondered what Belle would have thought about me going to an open air ceremony with a bunch of witches.

There I was, holding hands in a circle with four ladies dressed in black robes and hoods. The fire smoldered and crackled in the center of the circle. All their faces in shadow, hidden from me.

Kate's voice sounded like it rose from the Earth itself. She called the directions.

North and south, east and west. She brought all of creation into the circle. I felt dizzy, but alive. This was no place for a former pastor to be, hobnobbing with pagans.

Was it?

The wind came through, billowing up the flames. Heat wrapped around my face.

A crow flew over my head, so close I heard the air rustle over its feathers.

Belle?

She used to go outside, sit on the grass. For hours sometimes, just sitting. I'd ask her what she was doing. She said
she was in church. Then she'd laugh.

Crazy Belle.

Where was she?

Kate stepped forward. She picked up her broom. The one I
made not six hours before. She lifted it high over her head and
waved it back and forth like a giant metronome. I had the idea
she was brushing the sky. Sweeping it.

The other three ladies raised arms.

Mine felt heavy. Like they were carrying baskets full of
stones. But you know, after a while, they didn't seem that
heavy. I needed to lift my arms, too.

So I did. I reached about as high as I could go. I stretched
so I stood on my toes.

Kate brought the broom down close to me. She brushed the
air all around me, following my shape. She said some words.
I couldn't make them out. They were murmurs, maybe no
words at all, really, just the sound of the world.

Then things started getting darker. The sun had slipped
away. The stars were coming out. Below me the town was
turning on its lights, but they seemed so dim, like I was looking through sunglasses.

And Kate kept waving the broom around me.

The other ladies pulled back their hoods, one at a time.
Then I saw: They were all Belle. The first one was Belle when
we got married. Young. We were kids. Didn't know nothing.
The second one was Belle older, like when she used to sit on
the grass all the time. The third lady was Belle just before she

died. Those deep eyes. Understanding everything.

Kate brought the bristles close to me.

Their tips brushed against my clothes.

I felt the sharpness of the ends on my skin. Not enough to hurt, but enough to dig out—something.

Like she was bristling away cobwebs.

Then things started getting not just dark, but cloudy. The three Belles started wavering, like they were made of watercolors. Stained air. I couldn't see much through the haze that dropped over me.

I thought about Belle.

She used to love my brooms.

Loved to be in the shed with me. Loved the smell of the broomcorn. Liked to hold it in her hands. Laughing at the feel of it. Used to say how much she admired me for making brooms. For making witches feel at home in the world.

I'd never thought about it before. Figured it was one of Belle's jokes.

Where was she? What world?

Just before everything went completely dark, I thought I felt her. All around me.

Then nowhere.

"Hey."

Familiar voice. I knew who that was.

"Hey, Dwayne? What you doing here?"

I looked up at the sky. It was blocked by Harold, the sheriff. Half of Grangeville's law enforcement department. A halo glowed around him. Morning light.

"Uh," I said.

"You been out here all night, Dwayne?"

I sat up. My head felt thick, like it had been pumped full of dough.

"I guess so."

"You okay?"

I looked around. No sign of Kate or Belle. I stood and examined the ground, walking all over the top of the hill. Harold watched me with narrow eyes. Real suspicious like.

Absolutely no sign of a recent fire. Not one from last night at least.

"Just out for a walk, Dwayne?" said Harold. "Is that it?"

Over there, just past the rise. Was it?

I walked briskly toward the crooked stick.

The broom.

I picked it up and hefted it in my hands.

Harold was right next to me. "That what you were looking for?" he said. "This broom?"

"Yeah," I said.

"Not one of your better ones," said Harold.

I looked around the world. Grangeville spread out below me. A new day coming up.

My house was down there a bit. I could see the roof.

And I knew there was no one in it.

Not me or Belle.

"What would you say," I asked Harold, "if I told you this was the best broom I've ever made in my life?"

Harold took off his hat and scratched his head.

"Well, Dwayne. I'd have to say you were a little nuts in the head. Like maybe you went off your rocker just a little bit."

"Yes," I said. "I think you're right, Harold. Just a little bit."

Listening for the General
Kim Antieau

I hear the General below, his shears squeaking open and shut, open and shut, as I search his upstairs room. The noise stops, and I pause. Ice hits crystal, a familiar, penetrating sound, and I know Susano has brought the General his glass of water with lime. I open drawers, peer behind potted ferns, run a broom under the bed. If anyone passes by, I will become the old cleaning woman everyone sees when they look at me, harmless and above suspicion.

The shears open and close again. I glance outside. Pink petaled flowers fall slowly to the ground, brushing the General's shoes silently. I smile. He oils the shears often, and I wipe the oil away: I want his shears to be like the bell around a cat's neck. I hear footsteps downstairs. I push the broom back and forth on the beige and burgundy rug, sending dust into the air. But no one comes.

The shears stop. The outside spigot creaks open. Water splashes tile as the General washes the garden from his hands before his swim. "Susano!" he calls. Footsteps. Soft grunts as the General undresses. I imagine him balanced on the edge of the turquoise-tiled pool. The sound of his body hitting the water is startling, like a watermelon striking concrete.

I complete my search, finding nothing. I have been in the General's house for a month; still, I know little more about him than when I arrived. He has few visitors and corresponds with no one. Yet I have heard my people screaming in the mountains because of him. I have watched them die of wounds I could not heal. It is said a traitor whispers our secrets to the General.

I have found no traitor, but I will not return to my village until I do.

The General laughs and splashes once, and then the day falls silent again.

The howlers whistle in the amanta tree like possessed children. A breeze twists its way through the tangled gray branches of the enormous tree, becoming an eerie accompaniment to the monkeys. The General stands in the clearing, staring up at the moon whose light washes away the color of his face and clothes. He is silent, yet when the howlers stop for a moment, I think I can hear him breathing the jasmine-perfumed air.

I wonder if he talks to the moon. Perhaps she is the one who tells him the plans of my people; perhaps she urges him

to slice away the ear of an enemy or to leave boys disembow-
eled for the pigs to eat.

The turkeys do not sleep this night. Deep clicking sounds come from their throats as they pick worms and insects off tobacco leaves. A pig shuffles in the dirt. I turn from the General and look at the mountains blackened with night. In those mountains, my people now sleep, dreaming of times they have never known. Their dreams whisper to me, touching my ears with longings for the General's death. Yet his death would only speed along the advancement of another general, some-one worse perhaps; and still we would not know who betrays us. I hear the General come toward me. I do not move. I could end him now with the knife I have hidden in the folds of my skirt. I remain still.

"What are you doing, old woman?" he asks, his voice low, the sound moving up from his chest. These are the first words he has spoken to me.

I turn to him and smile my old woman smile.

"Listening to the music of the howlers, General," I say. "I hope I have not disturbed you."

He stares at me for a moment and then looks at the amanta tree.

"Music? You call that screeching music?" he asks, star-ing at the ghost-colored branches. He shakes his head. "No, you have not disturbed me. There are traitors everywhere, so I must be careful. You listen to monkeys? Well, listen for me, old woman, listen for the traitors."

The howlers are quiet, and I wonder if they understand us.

"I am an old woman," I say, "and sometimes I cannot even

hear my own thoughts."

He laughs and the howlers imitate him. His laughter dies away and he looks back at the tree, squinting.

"Someday I shall shoot them all," he says, and then his feet bend the dry grass, making it crackle like fire licking tender branches as he walks back toward the house.

Through the chink in the door I observe the woman from the city sitting across from the General. She sips champagne quietly. The General drinks his champagne continuously; the sound is like a pig with its nose buried deep in the stomach of a corpse. The light from the chandelier cleanses the room and accents the woman's diamonds and white satin dress. She is very young. I hear a clicking sound, and when I lean forward from my hiding place on the stairway, I see the General tapping his medals with the nails of his right hand.

"Most people believe I received these because I was either brave or brutal," he says. His knife scrapes across his plate as he cuts into his steak. "Both are true, of course, but not important. What is important to my success is that I have not forgotten the ways of the old ones. The rebels and terrorists in the mountains talk about getting their people food and putting shoes on their children's feet. It is all nonsense. The children are better off with their feet in contact with the Earth. They should be grateful to me. I could be harder on them, but I am not an extremist. I am able to keep order for the President by making only occasional raids. I am able to keep order because I remember the ways of our people. Others would be wise to remember the old ones, too.

"I will show you," he says. The cupboard door creaks slightly, sounding like the General's yawn as it moves open. Paper crinkles. The woman picks up the nutcracker—I see her rings flash as she reaches across the table. She places the nut between the metal bars, and then the shell cracks into a million pieces that scratch my ears, bringing my nightmare into this waking time. I close my eyes and the sound reverberates. I hear my nephew's screams again as the machete descends on him and slices through cartilage. His ear drops to the ground in an almost inaudible swoosh. I hear the smile in the General's voice as he orders one of his men to pick up the ear. I wait behind bamboo walls, listening to my own breath and the moans of my nephew until the sound of hooves dies away. The woman cracks open another nut, and tears touch my cheeks.

I hear the rustling of paper again and then something drops into liquid. I lean forward. The General's holding a paper sack. Something brown, like a dried peach, floats in the woman's champagne.

"I know the ways of the old ones," he says, "and I listen well. They all wonder why I take only one ear, or why I do not kill all the men outright instead of taking an ear. They don't understand." He laughs; it is more like a gurgle, like someone choking in water. The woman has grown pale and her skin now matches her dress. "I hear everything if I listen closely enough. I hear their thoughts, I hear the moans of their lovers, I hear the secrets of their comrades. I even hear the worms eating them as they lie buried beneath the ground."

I move back into the darkness, not wanting to see the thing floating in the glass or hear it take in champagne like a sponge soaking up water.

How foolish we all were. We have called the General many things, but we never thought of him as one of us. We had forgotten he is of our race, he is a human being. I shudder. He is also someone who serves the old gods, an *ah-men*—or more likely, an *ah-pulyaah,* a practitioner of black magic. Or so the outsiders name it. His trick is an old one: if an *ah-pulyaah* takes an eye, he can see all that the other eye sees, if he takes a hand, he'll know what the other hand does. If he slices off an ear, it becomes a cornucopia of thoughts and sound.

The General comes to the door, and I press myself against the wall. The light is shut away as the door closes tightly. I stand and leave the house, my feet making no more sound than mist does as it settles on the tube roses. I hope the General does not hurt the woman from the city, but I am afraid he saw the fear in her eyes, just as I did.

I scrape bark from the amanta tree and drop the shavings into my bag. The howlers hiss at me. The night is quiet except for a faraway wind pushing trees against the mountainsides. Back in the darkened kitchen, I poke at the fire until it snaps at me, and then I boil the bark. The sounds of bubbles breaking fills the room. Then I wait for the liquid to cool. The house is silent as I stir honey into the bark. My father was an *ah-men* and I used to listen to his chants as a child. His words were not for female ears, and his black magic was something he practiced only occasionally. Yet I had listened. Later I sometimes used the knowledge when I was needed as a healer; the Lords of the Days always served me, apparently unaware of my sex.

I take the newly made *balché* out to the amanta tree, and there I drink it slowly. The turkeys pick, pick, pick. When the monkey howls turn to lullabies and the sun begins to rise, I take out my father's *zaztiin,* a clear stone ball given to him by his father, and I dip it in the *balché.* I chant softly.

The distant hills are bathed in smoky purple. The air surrounding the estate is tinged in gold. A car takes away the woman from the city. I hear her tears as they fall into her palm, like drops of water falling from the tallest tree in the rain forest to the forest floor. The General goes to the garden and begins his day. The shears squeak open and shut. A breeze brings the words of Susano to me as he asks Julia where the old woman is. Ice clicks against crystal. Water hits tile. The General laughs and splashes in the pool.

I drink *balché* and wait for the sun to drop again. When it is dark, the monkeys chatter noisily, as if to hide the sounds of my soles as I go into the kitchen. I drop a large portion of sleeping powder into the General's night drink just before Susano comes for it. Then I take a butcher knife from the kitchen and wait outside with the monkeys, sharpening the blade, until the house grows silent with sleep.

Ferns brush my cheeks as I walk up the stairs. Inside the General's room, I scratch matches against metal. The flame hisses and bursts gold. I light the lantern. The flame spits at me as it illuminates the General's face. I dab the skin around his ear with alcohol. He does not move.

I put the blade to his ear, and then swiftly, I force the knife down. For a moment, I hear sounds like a machete slicing through cornstalks; the room glows gold and I am not certain where I am, and then the ear falls away from the General's head. I watch black liquid stain the sheets and hear it seep into the linen like misty rain falling on soldier's fatigues. I wrap his head with bandages. The General moans once. I place his ear on one of his silk handkerchiefs. Then I pull out the *zaztiin* and wave it over the ear. The clear stone squeaks on its chain like the General's shears. My chants fill the house. I hear them travel outside where the monkeys repeat my words.

When I am certain the Lords of the Days have heard me, I wrap the ear in the handkerchief. I listen to the General's uneven breathing. Now we shall know his thoughts, too; his ear will be better than the warning bell on a cat. I go downstairs and get the paper sack from the dining room. The only sound is the crackling of the paper against my hand. I imagine the ears pressed against the sack, listening.

I leave the house and take a horse from the stables. I ride past the amanta tree where the monkeys click and past the tobacco field where the turkeys gobble worms. I hold the ear close to mine to hear the General's dreams. His dream sounds are empty—like splashes of water in a turquoise-tiled pool. The horse knows the mountain well and it carries me quickly toward my village. I am not afraid of the dark because I know the General's men do not come out at night. Insects snap at the ear, drawn to its sound like moths to a light. The General's dreams keep me company through the night.

The sun lights the sky as I arrive at my village. People gather round me, offering food and drink. I had not told any of them where I had gone. Now they question me. I listen to the ear, and the sounds of the General's screams come to me.

                                    KIM ANTIEAU

He has discovered his loss.

"This is the General's ear," I say, sliding off the horse.

"Only his ear, grandma?" one of the villagers says as I open the handkerchief. "Is he dead?"

I shake my head. "I have done better than kill him."

Suddenly everything becomes quiet. I look around. I hear tortillas sizzling, a dog barking, my horse's urine spraying the ground, yet it is quiet. I gaze down at the ear in my hand, and I realize I am no longer hearing the sounds which accompanied me to the village. The General is silent.

We hear news of the *Matanza*—the slaughter—long before it reaches us. The General is no longer content with taking parts of us, we are told; instead, he is killing us all. I wave my *zaztiin* over his shriveled ear and call up the Lords of the Days. They do not listen. The young people either laugh at me or curse me for letting the General live as they make preparations to leave their homes.

I am inside my hut when the General rides into the village. His horses breathe hard, sucking in the dusty day. The soldiers' guns bang against their legs, making a strange metallic thud. I peer through the bamboo walls. The General sits on his palomino, his head turned away from me. I can see the scar where I cut off his ear. It has healed nicely. He twists his head around. The other scar has not healed as well. It is ragged and red where he cut—or tore-off—his ear. Now I understand why the Lords did not hear my chants.

The General motions to his men and the screaming begins. As I run from my house, I hear his head move, the bones in his neck cracking, and I know he is looking at me.

"Old woman!" he screams, his words twisting into the howls of the monkeys who sit like ghosts in the old amanta tree. His words fill my ears as the sounds die all around me.

The Untied States of America
Mario Milosevic

Five Days Ago

I sighted land off the eastern cliff. I was doing a standard search of the water, part of my job. I stood on the edge of the precipice of my home state of Washington, the water lapping at the rocks a couple of thousand feet below me, a thin line of white marking the shoreline. There was a beach, of sorts, down there. I sometimes wanted to descend to it but never had the nerve. It would be an epic rock climb, something I was too old for anyway. An old woman. Good only for looking out to sea.

The air that morning was clear, and the sea was calm. No telling why another state drifted into range. I tried to see if it also had a white line at the water mark, but it was too far away to tell. Really, it was nothing more than a brown bump on the horizon. A tiny swelling.

A brisk wind snapped at my pants. I clutched my jacket tighter around my throat.

My estimate was at least 80 miles away. Which state was it? Who could tell? They all looked alike from this distance.

I had to inform my fellow travelers. Anytime a state comes into view, there is a danger of collision. So far, almost seventy years after the breakup, we have avoided crashing into any other state, but there was no guarantee our fortune would continue.

I needed to go back to sound the alert.

But something about seeing the other state held me to the edge of the cliff. It had been a couple years since the last incident. That time we came very close to another drifting state. I saw people waving at me from the other shore. I waved back. They cupped their hands to their mouths and shouted at me, but the sea air snatched their words away and I could not tell what they were saying. I shouted to them until I was hoarse, but I'm sure they could not hear me either. I watched them drift by. The currents of the open ocean are completely unpredictable.

I saw vegetation on the other state. It was low in the water, so I knew it wasn't a mountain state. Perhaps a coastal state like Florida? Perhaps.

In any case, it drifted to the north and I watched it wistfully, wondering if my son had made it there.

Before I Was Born

My grandmother helped with the breakup of the country. She was pregnant with my mother at the time. She lived in Eastern Washington state, right smack up against Idaho. When I was growing up I remember her saying something about people from Idaho. She didn't like them. She was glad they were now across an ocean and she didn't have to look at any of them. Never told me why. Maybe she never had a reason. In any case, she was only too happy to drop the pellets along the border.

You know about the pellets, don't you? They arrived in the mail of anyone living within fifty miles of a state line. Any state line, anywhere in the country. The instructions were clear. Take the pellets to the border and drop them there and leave them. Thousands, maybe millions of people did exactly that. My grandmother being one of them. The pellets cooked in the sun. This was August, when even Minnesota and Maine get sun. The pellets expanded, grew heavier, and sunk into the ground. As they went, they ate the earth.

There's no other way to describe it really. They chewed down through the crust of the earth until they got to the magma below.

The breakup was just that simple. No one knows where the pellets came from, or what they were made of. If you want to know the truth, I'm not even sure there *were* pellets, but that's how the story has come down to us, so who am I to argue with it?

Those first few days must have been amazing. The sound of rocks splitting, rivers falling over cliffs into the wounds between the states. Steam rising as the water touched the magma and filled in the spaces between the states.

Imagine planes in the air at the time, looking to land at an airport, when suddenly the airport is not where it's supposed to be because the city, stuck on top of a floating state, has moved under the plane.

Within a few days there was no contiguous land between Mexico and Canada, just some 48 gigantic barges made of rock, slowly moving into the Pacific and Atlantic oceans.

We were no longer the United States of America. We had become a roaming group of isolated islands, each one independent of the other, with roads and bridges that once crossed state lines now nothing but broken metal, concrete, and asphalt hanging off the cliffs like rags. Mountains were cut in two. Plains neatly bisected. Forests split up like divorcing families.

Most rivers were completely drained within a day. They simply emptied off the top edge and tumbled into the water below. With no connection to neighboring states, rivers could not replenish. State governments immediately saw that water would be an issue in the new reality of the Untied States of America. Rationing measures became the order of the day.

Gas and oil pipelines broke, spilling into the ocean. Communication lines were severed. Anything that crossed a state line was broken. Each state became an isolated entity unto itself.

All this happened years before I was born. My mother told me about it, even though it happened before *she* was born. She talked about the old country like it was something she still wanted. Like it was something she had once lived in. She wanted to be attached to the other states.

But that would never happen. Not anymore. You can't put the pieces back together.

Four Days Ago

I informed my fellow Washingtonians, as was my duty, by calling the central government agency and carefully describing what I saw. The voice on the other end of the line was skeptical.

"We haven't had a sighting in 28 months," he said.

"I know," I said.

"Are you sure about this?"

"Of course."

He made a noise I could not decipher. "A lot of people think all the other states crashed or sank."

"I don't know why they would think that," I said. "We haven't crashed or sunk."

"Go out there again," he said.

"I'm telling you I know what I saw," I said, now irritated with his attitude.

"Go," he said. "We need corroborative evidence anyway."

"I can't corroborate my own sighting."

"Just go."

He hung up. I didn't go that day; I was in too much of a sulk. Besides, it was almost dark by then. I woke the next morning before dawn and walked to the edge of the cliff and waited for the sun to come up and illuminate the water. I strained my eyes, in the darkness, to see lights. Surely Florida, or whatever state it might be, had lights, just as we did. But I saw nothing. Maybe the man on the other end of the line was right. Maybe I imagined seeing land in the ocean.

I sighed. Was my own history betraying me? Perhaps, perhaps. I only knew that I wanted to see land. Yearned to. We were not meant for this life. We should never have separated. The breakup was the biggest mistake in history. I hated that a member of my own family had taken part in it.

Such were my thoughts as the wind, cold and wet, swirled around me. The sky began to lighten. I stood up and watched the world come to life. There were whitecaps in the ocean. We had been drifting north for some time, catching a current into colder climates. Crops, under stress at the best of times, with the natural rhythm of the seasons completely out of whack, were straining under the conditions. The entire state had been put on food rationing, in anticipation of possible shortages.

As the sun rose into the sky, flooding the water and my state with illumination, I saw that the land I saw the day before was gone. We had drifted apart.

I felt so much disappointment that I could barely contain my grief. I cried. I stood on the lip of the state and cried. I could not even tell what I was crying for. A united state that I had never experienced? A nostalgia for a past that seemed brighter than this present? Silly sentimental thoughts. They were not worthy of me.

Do you want to know how I know I am right about the folly of the breakup? Simple. No one lives where I live. I am alone. After the breakup people moved inland, as close to the center of Washington as possible. They didn't want to see the ocean.

They didn't want to be presented with the stark evidence of their isolation.

In any case, as the breakup was happening, immense earthquakes shook our state. Tall buildings in downtowns toppled. Entire cities became nothing but shattered wrecks. It was best to move to the rural center anyway.

But some, people like me, remained on the edges. A network of us watchers, scanning the horizon for evidence of close encounters.

I was not sure that others were doing their jobs. Why had no one else reported seeing the land? It was long and distant enough that another watcher would have seen it.

You see my situation? I could not accuse anyone else of not doing their job. That would be unkind and unprofessional. But the evidence was clear.

I strained my eyes even more. I shielded my face from the glare of the sun.

No land, but something else. A dot.

Far off in the ocean, a speck of *something*, floating on the water and heading in my direction. I leaned forward. It looked like a small boat. It had that fish shape. I thought I saw oars paddling the water on either side, like a water bug skimming the surface of the water.

And finally, after straining my eyes so much I thought they would pop: I believed that I discerned a figure. A person operating the oars.

My spine tingled. Someone from the other state was coming here. To Washington. I could barely contain my excitement.

After I Was Born

I asked my grandmother once, when I was twelve and she was eighty, decades after the breakup, why she did it. Why did she obey some crazy instructions she got in the mail?

She didn't want to answer me. How could she? It made no sense. Even to a twelve year old, it made no sense. Maybe especially to a twelve year old. At that age, you are finely attuned to bullshit.

"Susie," she said, "it was a crazy time. We were ready to try anything to make it better."

I remember thinking: *This was better? All the states floating around in the ocean out of sight of each other was better?*

"You'll have to explain that one to me, Gramma," I said.

Now imagine her in a rocking chair with a corncob pipe in her mouth, staring up at the sky and composing an answer for her precocious granddaughter. That's not how it was, but that's how I have come to remember it after all these years. My grandmother's gone and I still have an active imagination and that's how I remember her. That's how I like to imagine her.

"Are there people in your school you don't like?" she said.

"Sure," I said.

"Why?"

I shrugged. "Well, Walter is mean, and Gayle doesn't like *me* so why should I like *her*, and Ingrid likes boys way too much to be friends with me so I'm not friends with her."

                                          MARIO MILOSEVIC

"That's how it was with us in those days. Most of the states couldn't get along. We wanted to be independent of each other."

"Excuse me, Gramma," I said, "but that is just plain crazy. You don't cut yourself off from the rest of the country just because you don't get along."

"Looking back on it," she said, "you're completely right. But we didn't see it that way. We thought the pellets were the answer to our problems. Independence." She stared at me with open eyes, like she was daring me to talk back to her, which didn't make a lot of sense right then because I had no desire to defy her. I just wanted to know the story. The real story.

"What happened after the pellets ate the borders?" I said.

My grandmother looked at the sky. Like she was trying to decide if I was old enough to hear the real story. She must have concluded that I was.

"We didn't expect the destruction," she said. "Now I wonder how stupid we could have been. Many people died. Buildings collapsed. Fires everywhere. It was awful. We were mostly away from all of that. We didn't hear about it until later, but we saw the smoke in the air. The ground shook. It just rattled. I was afraid it was going to break my bones, to tell you the truth. It didn't, but I still think it could have. It took days for things to come to some kind of order again. So much destruction. Your grandfather died, did you know that? He was at work when the breakup happened. He sold cars. He was in his office when the roof caved in on him and killed him. Oh, Susie, it was awful. More than awful. We all felt terrible. But it was like we were under some kind of spell. When your mother was born five months later, it was a completely different world. The state was floating in the ocean, just like all the other states. Our population was much smaller. We spent a lot of time burying the dead. And things were primitive. We couldn't communicate with the other states. We wanted them back, but it was too late. I turned all my attention to your mother. I wanted her to have the best possible life she could have, especially since we had torn her world apart."

She told me what she had to tell me, and I knew she would never say it again, so I tried to remember it as best I could.

"You never married again?" I asked my grandmother.

"It wasn't something I wanted," she said. "All I could think of was your mother. She became my life."

Three Days Ago

Do you ever walk barefoot? You, reading this, I'm asking if you walk barefoot. Think about it.

I don't mean in your house or apartment. I mean outside. Letting your feet touch the ground.

It's not a bad way to spend some time. It's about the only way to get to know the land you live on. If you don't let your soles come in contact with dirt, you're like the orphan who doesn't know who his parents were.

The day after I saw the boat and the figure in the water, I watched the sun come up over the ocean. I stepped out of my house, put my bare feet on the ground, and walked toward the light. I went a mile or so over grass and mud, and stopped at the edge where the cut had been made. The sky was lit up pretty good. I looked across the water, hoping to catch a glimpse of the lone sailor. No luck this morning. I floated on the molten core of the planet, along with the rest of the state, which gave a peculiarly solid, yet lonely feeling.

So the sailor was gone? Just like that?

I felt lost. I had never met the person and yet I was devastated by his absence. How could such a thing be?

I looked down at the shoreline. The waves moved in slow motion from this distance, as if they were memories or dream sequences. No sound. The waves broke on the rocks, had to, but I heard nothing. There was driftwood down there. And shells, no doubt. All the items that make a beach.

I strained my eyes again, narrowed my eyelids to block out the glare of the sun and discerned a small dark speck at the intersection of blue and white.

The boat I saw yesterday was beached.

Now where was its occupant?

I scanned the beach line carefully but saw nothing. Then I turned my attention to the rock face, the cliff that had been carved out by my grandmother and her cohorts. The cleaving had not been a perfect thing. There were ruts and breaks in the rock. Over the years, grass and bushes—even small trees— had found anchor there, pushing their roots into the exposed rock. Cormorants and sea gulls had built nests, creating settlements of their own. Down at the bottom of the cliff, near the beach, I detected a small motion. I moved to the side to get a different angle on it, to ensure I was not fooling myself.

I was not. The figure from the boat was definitely climbing up the face of the cliff.

I put out my hand and waved to him. I shouted. "Hello!"

He made no indication that he heard me. Well, he probably *didn't* hear me. How could he, so far down and with the wind swirling around him? Not to mention the sound of seagulls as they carved arcs in the air.

How long would it take him to climb the cliff? I had no idea. A day? An hour?

A day seemed closer to the truth. He was starting out at first light. He probably needed to get up here before dark. Did I have time to inform the network?

I decided there was time, but also, on the spot, decided there was no reason to tell. This was going to be my secret, at least for the time being.

I stretched out, belly on the grass, so my head was just over the precipice. I stared down at the man (I was pretty sure now that he was a male) and watched, mesmerized by his progress, which seemed so slow. Silently I cheered him on. I wanted him to get here. I wanted to meet him.

He climbed steadily and took only small rests. The day wore on. The sun grew hot. I was uncomfortable and could only imagine how he must be doing.

About mid-afternoon I thought to get some food for when he got to the top, but I did not want to leave my spot on the cliff. I did not want to break contact—however tenuous—with him. It was as if by leaving my place he would disappear. So I didn't move.

He still had about a third of the way to go and the sun was creeping toward the horizon when he stopped. He looked up. I waved at him and shouted.

"Are you all right?"

He waved back. "I'm fine," he shouted back. His voice seemed small.

"Who are you?"

"A friend," he said. "There's a small cave here. I'm going to spend the night."

He disappeared into a grotto out of my view. I watched the spot in the fading sun until it was completely lost in the darkness.

After I Was Married

My grandmother died and my son was born. The three of us, my child, my husband, and me, moved to the edge of the state. My parents were upset by this development. They wanted us to live near them in the interior, but my husband had some peculiar ideas about the world. He wanted to see the ocean, he said. The water, so much of it, appealed to his sense of adventure. He wanted to know the full extent of the world and he could know that only by living near the sea.

After the breakup, Washington state—and all the others I had to assume—bobbed up in the water, raised itself like a balloon floating in the air. It was as though the land reached up for the skies when it had been severed from the rest of the states. When I was younger and my grandmother told me about this, I thought it was wonderful, a marvelous development that turned us all into exalted beings, reaching for the stars.

That was when I was younger. As I grew up, I began to think of the rising as a curse. It created towering cliffs all along our state, further isolating us from the world by making the ocean a perilous climb away in which one had to risk one's life to traverse the cliff face. There are some, however, who relish the view from on high. My husband was one of them.

For many years I refused to go near the edge of the state. I knew we were a floating land mass. I did not need to be reminded of it. But my husband went out every day. He walked for hours along the cliff edge and after a while I noticed that when he returned from these visits he was always happier than when he left. I wondered what could be so marvelous about seeing the ocean everyday. It was just a featureless expanse of blue.

Since we lived on the edge, we became part of the network of edge watchers charged with looking for drifting states that might collide with us. They strung a line out to our house and installed a phone, the height of modernity on our little island, and we took to making daily reports. My husband did the observing on the edge and I made the reports. Mostly I called in and said the ocean was clear. Occasionally my husband would see other states, always a long way off. We dutifully reported these sightings and imagined that someone on the other end was taking down all the information and using it to track the comings and goings, the *meanderings*, of the various states that once made up our country. I supposed this was a valuable thing to do and accepted our role in helping to make it accurate and true.

That is what finally brought me out to the cliffs: the sense of duty to my state. I brought my son with me. He was less than a year old, not even named yet, when he first saw the ocean. I walked slowly up to the edge and stopped some ten feet from

                                    MARIO MILOSEVIC

it. My husband was with me. He strode right to the edge. My heart leaped in my throat. How could he be so casual?

"How far down is it?" I asked. The wind caught my words and tossed them over the edge. Or so it seemed to me.

He shrugged. "A long way. You wouldn't want to fall." He grinned. I was shaking with fear.

"Please step back from the edge," I said.

He did as I asked, though reluctantly. My son, cradled in my arms, pushed at me with his feet. He wanted to get closer to the water, I could see that. He reached for the ocean with his hand, clenching and unclenching his fist. His eyes were on the water. His entire being was enraptured with the beauty of it.

Or so it seemed to me.

Looking back, I think this was the precise moment when I lost him.

Two Days Ago

I didn't spend the night on the cliff. Instead I went back to my house and spent a restless night wondering what was going to happen the next day. Several times I began to pick up the phone to report what I had seen, but I always put it back in its cradle. I had this peculiar notion that the man was nobody's business but mine.

I did not sleep well and woke up hours before the sun and prepared food for him. I got cheese and jerky, some biscuits and boiled eggs and put them in a basket and headed back to the cliff. The air was chilly but there was little wind. The sea sounded calm. I sat near the place where I had been the night before. When the sky lightened up enough, I looked over the edge. The man was not there. I waited. Seagulls called out, filling the air with sadness. Sometimes the cries of gulls make me think of my son. He loved seeing them. Would chase after them sometimes. I knew he wanted to leap off the edge of the cliff and fly with them. Knew it from the time he was too young to walk.

As the sky grew less dark and the light of the sun began to paint the cliff, I saw the man poke his head out of his cave.

"Ahoy!" I called to him.

He looked up and waved. "Ahoy!" he said, and grinned. I was glad the wind had died down this morning. I could hear the man.

"Did you sleep well?" I asked.

"Well enough under the circumstances."

"I have food for you."

"Oh good. You're too kind."

"Where are you from?"

"My barge was Vermont."

A small state, then. Or smaller than most. I made a note to tell my superiors.

"Why did you leave it?" I asked.

"No reason," said the man. "I wanted some adventure."

Well, I guess he found it. Rowing across the open ocean and ending up on this cliff. But I didn't quite believe him, either. Someone needed more than a sense of adventure to risk their life like this. Didn't they?

"What's your name?" I asked.

He had pulled himself completely out of his cave and was

beginning to climb up toward me. I saw that he had a water bottle strapped to his back, but nothing else. Which meant, unless he captured and consumed a cormorant or a seagull last night, he hadn't eaten in some time.

"My name is Clay," he said.

"I'm Susan," I said.

"Glad to meet you," he said, "in a couple of hours."

I pulled back from the edge. In a couple of hours? Sure. I was glad to have talked to him, but I still didn't know anything about him.

I went back to my house and called my contact.

"I have a visitor," I said.

"Visitor?" He sounded as irritated with me as ever.

"He's climbing up the cliff. He came from the land mass I reported earlier. Vermont."

"How do you know it was Vermont?"

"The visitor told me."

"Put the visitor on the phone."

"I can't. He's not here yet."

The voice on the line hesitated. "Don't waste my time," he said. And hung up.

I called him back. "Don't do that," I said. "I'm telling you the truth. He's climbing up the cliff and will be here soon."

Silence.

"Hello?" I said.

"We'll send someone out," said the voice. Then he hung up again. Fine. I was going to have assistance. But it would take a while for anyone to get to my house. I called some of the other edge watchers along the cliff. I told them the situation. They were ecstatic. A visitor to our state. How marvelous.

Yes. Well. Maybe marvelous and maybe not.

I returned to the cliff and looked over. The man was much closer. He climbed with an efficiency and sense of purpose I admired. Even though I could see only the top of his head, I saw that he was a man of energy. He looked to be about the age my son would have been. Or maybe not. Maybe I was making him my son's age because I wanted him to *be* my son. The brain can do such strange things sometimes.

As he got closer to the rim, I slid over to the side. He gripped the edges of the rock with his fingers. I marveled that he did not slip and fall, for if he had, he would surely have died, broken on the beach below.

As he got closer I heard his breathing. Powerful gulps of air. His clothes rustled in the silence. I thought of my son. How he had such strength and will so early in his life. How that will changed everything for us.

Clay put his hands over the top. His fingers touched grass and he extended his grip, then pulled himself up and over the edge and flopped down on the ground. He rolled over and stared up at the sky, then began laughing.

"I thought I would never make it," he said.

I walked over to him and stood with the basket of food. "Well," I said, "you did make it. Welcome to Washington."

He got up on his feet and tried to look serious, but the grin would not leave his face. He nodded to me and bowed slightly. "Very happy to make your acquaintance," he said. "I hope I'm not intruding."

"Not at all," I said. "Would you like some food?"

                    MARIO MILOSEVIC

He took the basket with perhaps a little more force than he wanted to and opened it. "Oh my," he said. "I haven't seen cheese in ages."

"Really?" I said. I remembered from my grandmother's lessons that Vermont had been a cheese producer before the breakup.

"The cows in Vermont all died a long time ago."

"Really?"

Clay nodded. He took up a piece of jerky and bit into it. He obviously relished it. "Vermont drifted into the arctic latitudes for a while. It was so cold for so long that most everything died. Animals, trees, even grass. We had no summer for years and there was no time to adapt. We have become very primitive. Much more primitive than before the breakup. Then a few years ago the currents took us in a more southerly direction, but things haven't come back. No one knows if they ever will."

He sounded sad, telling me about his home. Was it all just random chance, what happened to one's home state?

"I stand on the cliffs and watch for other states," I said. "I have never seen anyone leave their state to come to another."

"Yes, I would expect not," he said. "Not many do what I have done. Some, but very few."

I didn't tell him about my son. Instead I indicated the path back to my house. "I would be happy to let you stay at my place for a time," I said.

"That would be lovely," he said. He extended his arm to me and I took his elbow and we walked back to my house.

The seagulls and the ocean receded behind us. The sun

warmed our path. Grassy fields extended all around us.

"Oh, this is lovely," said Clay. "I had no idea things were like this on other states."

"Vermont is not like this?" I said.

He shook his head. "Vermont has become a wasteland. We have very few people left. Those that remain are sick. I had to leave, you see. I had to know if other states were better off."

That was disheartening. I had hoped that other states were as well preserved as Washington. I wanted to think that all of the states were thriving. Now it appeared this was not so.

We got to the house and I showed him to a small room in the back where I had set up a small cot, anticipating that he would want to spend a night or two.

"I hope this is not too primitive for you," I said.

"Oh," he said. "Not at all."

"There will be people coming tomorrow."

"People?"

"I informed others. They will be curious. You will be something of a celebrity."

He seemed to consider this. It did not appear to trouble him, only to amuse him. "A celebrity? Well. I don't think I know how to be a celebrity."

"I wouldn't worry about that," I said. "I imagine you will just need to be yourself."

"Excellent advice," said Clay. "I will strive for that."

He looked so tired. I wanted to ask him more about Vermont, but he could barely keep his eyes open. I told him he could rest as long as he wanted; then I closed the door on his room.

　　　　　　　　　　　　　　　　

After the Funeral

I had nightmares that tore my heart to pieces. I saw my son go over the edge and fall to the ocean below, in slow motion. I reached for his hand. He reached for mine. We strained toward each other, but could never touch. Always out of reach and him falling falling. He never touched the water, but I could never save him either. We were in an in-between place where neither of us could do anything, an eternal limbo of futility, more frightening and soul draining than it would have been to see him smashed against the rocks below.

I always woke from such dreams with sweat covering my body and my heart thumping against my chest. I called for my son. Called his name and he came running into my room. Sixteen years old. No time for bullshit but still feeling duty bound toward his mother.

"Mom," he said. "You're dreaming again."

Yes. I was dreaming again. I wanted his father here. My husband.

"I'm okay," I said, in a shaky voice that conveyed the exact opposite.

"Was it Dad?" he said. "Were you dreaming of Dad?"

I was not, but how could I tell him I was dreaming of his prolonged death? Impossible.

"Yes," I said.

"I miss him too," he said. "But he's gone."

He had been gone for months. No one's fault, not really. How could I blame anyone? He had been on the edge, peering out at the sea, catching sight of land. Another state floating in the distance. The air was wet with fog. He wanted a closer look. He stepped forward, a few steps too many.

I was there with him. I saw him turn in the air. Startled expression for one second. Less than that. An instant. Hardly long enough to catch each other's eye. Maybe we did. It's hard to remember now, hard to know what happened and what I merely *wanted* to happen. Then he disappeared. Simply dropped from view. I ran to the edge. Saw him cartwheeling in the air. Hitting the cliff. Not believing any of it. It didn't happen. Wasn't happening. I closed my eyes because I knew I didn't want the final image in my brain. Kept them closed for a long long time.

"Yes," I said to my son. "He's gone. But you're here."

He looked away. Ready to be gone. So soon? My son didn't want to be near me?

"I have breakfast," he said.

"I'm not hungry."

"You have to eat."

I made myself get out of bed. Four months since my husband's death, and I had not been to the edge. My son had been taking care of my duties, scanning the horizon, looking for land. Why? Who cared if there was land out there?

My son had laid out an impressive breakfast. He must have gotten up early. I felt a certain dread in my heart.

"What's this?" I said.

"You need to eat more," he said. "I made pancakes and sausage. You like sausage."

"Yes," I said. I sat at the table and picked at the food on my plate but did not taste any of it.

"Well," he said.

"Well what?"

"Aren't you going to eat any of it?"

"Why did you make this for me? You never make breakfast."

"I can make breakfast." Proud. Defiant? Maybe.

"I know you *can*," I said. "You just never *do*."

"I think you need to get back to your duties," he said.

"My duties?"

"Mom," he said, "you can't just spend your days wishing Dad was back."

I didn't. At least, I didn't think I did. I had the nightmares, yes, but that was nothing. Just grief. Completely understandable. I felt like I needed to be strong for my son. He had spent so much time with his dad. Well, they both spent time away from me. Lived for the edge. Abandoned me to the house and the chickens and the sheep if truth be told, but I never begrudged them each other. They were men. They needed each other's company.

And now that one of them was gone, the other was forced to find company with me. It was not a good fit. Not in any way.

"I can wish anything I want," I said. My own defiance. Defiance to my son. How ridiculous. And yet, how right it felt.

"I was thinking," said my son.

Here it came.

"Thinking?"

"That maybe I need to get away from here. For a while."

I had expected something like that. He was of an age when

he needed to find his own way in the world. What was left of it.

"You want to go inland?" I said. "That's fine with me. You should see what our island state is like. It'll do you good."

He leaned back in his chair, scowling.

"What?" I said.

"I don't mean here, on Washington. I mean out there." He hooked a thumb toward the window, but he obviously meant more than outside the window. He was talking about the open ocean.

When your child decides to leave you, that is supposed to be a wonderful day, so I have been told. You've fulfilled your duty as a parent: you have given your child wings. I didn't feel wonderful at that moment. Or any moment since.

"You can't go," I said.

"I've already got a boat."

"But where? Where will you go?"

"What does it matter? I just want to get off this floating nothing."

"There are only other floating nothings. That's all the world is, a collection of floating land masses. Why risk your life to go to another when you have this one right here?"

"You don't understand," he said.

Of course. How could I? I wasn't a teenager anymore. I didn't have that yearning he had.

"You should find a girlfriend," I said. "That would cure you of this nonsense." I had in mind the daughter of another land watcher, just up the edge a bit. She would be perfect for my son. I would love to have her as a daughter-in-law in a few years.

"Mom!"

"What?"

"That's not what this is about."

"No," I said. "I suppose it isn't. I will never have grand-children, will I?"

He looked disgusted. When did I begin to disgust my own child? "I don't ever want children. I don't want to raise them in this world."

"And yet, you want to see this world."

He had no answer for that. I had no follow up, no longer any desire to debate the point with him. Our breakfasts grew cold on our plates.

"I'm leaving today," he said.

"Fine," I said. "Do you have a proper boat?"

"Yes. I lowered one down the cliff already."

Ah. He'd been busy then, doing more than looking out for rogue states. "Have you seen any other land masses?"

"Some."

"Can I come see you off?"

He hesitated. I felt an awful smugness at his hesitation, like I had won something.

"If you really want to," he said.

I wasn't sure I did.

Yesterday

I did the arithmetic in my head: My visitor looked to be in his early twenties. Call it twenty-two, although he might have been even younger. My son left twenty-four years ago. Which meant he could have landed on another state, gotten married and had a son of his own within two years of his departure. Sure. It was very possible.

In the morning I peeked in on the visitor. He was still asleep. I studied his peaceful face for some sign of a family resemblance, but found nothing that suggested me or my husband or my son. I knew if I stared long enough I would begin to see family traits that weren't there, so I quietly closed the door and went outside to take in the morning sun. It burned the air. It heated my skin but not enough. I wanted it to sear me to charcoal. How could I think this man was my grandson? After all this time? How could I think that my own son had somehow survived to make a life and a family for himself?

Hope springs eternal. The curse of humans everywhere.

"Hey there, Susie." A male voice behind me.

I turned around.

It was Weaver, an edge watcher from up the coast, arriving on foot. I had seen him a few times, but mostly he stayed to himself, like most of the edge watchers. He must have walked twenty miles.

"What are you doing here?" I said.

"Heard about the visitor. Where is he?"

"Asleep at my house."

"Come on," he said "Let's go wake him."

I was reluctant to do so. I wanted to hold onto my fantasy a little longer. I knew a few well chosen questions would destroy the illusion I had so carefully constructed for myself. Weaver stood looking at me. He was old, like I was, and had that slow kind of motion to him, the way we get. The world too much

　MARIO MILOSEVIC

for us. The whole heavy wheel of it crushing us down. But there was something else in him. An excitement, like maybe this visitor was some kind of salvation. Was that it?

"Okay," I said. "Let's go wake him."

"Have you been to any other states?" Weaver asked.

We were all sitting at my kitchen table. Breakfast on plates in front of us. Clay eating like there was no tomorrow. I forgot how much young people can put away. I wondered if I had served him enough.

"No," he said to Weaver. "This is my first trip."

Weaver sounded disappointed. "So you don't know anything about any other states?"

"A little. Some have visited Vermont. They have stories to tell."

I perked up. "My grandson took off a long time ago," I said. "Do you think he came to Vermont?"

"How long?" said Clay.

"Over twenty years."

"Don't think so," said Clay. "My dad told me we hadn't gotten visitors for a long time before the first one he remembers. What was his name?"

I told him.

"Doesn't ring a bell at all," said Clay. "Why did he leave Washington?"

I shrugged. "Why did you leave Vermont?"

"Indeed," said Weaver. "What made you leave?"

"I wanted to see the world."

"Washington isn't the world," said Weaver.

"It's a part of it," said Clay, suddenly sounding unsure of himself. I wondered if he wanted more than he found here. Did he think other states were going to be so much more grand than his own home?

"I think," I said, "what Weaver is trying to say, is what do you think of our little piece of the country?"

"Yes," said Weaver. "Now that you're here, was it worth it? Are you glad you left? It must have been a scary trip."

"There were some moments," said Clay. "The seas were rough. But you know, Vermont is nothing. It's just getting bleaker all the time. People who come to Vermont, they leave right away."

"Really?" said Weaver.

Clay nodded. "Oh, sure. They leave a desolate state and end up in Vermont and see it is no different and move on to another. We've had visitors from Montana, Arizona, Ohio, and Colorado. All pretty depressing places now."

"But there's all kinds of states you haven't had visitors from, right?" said Weaver.

"Yeah. We figure those are the nice places. The ones that people don't want to leave."

"Exactly the conclusion I would have reached," said Weaver.

I listened and tried to take in the conversation, but mostly I had lost interest. None of this mattered, not really. We were still on Washington, and it still seemed like a perfectly acceptable place to be living. Why would anyone want to leave it? Why would my son?

We finished our breakfasts and then I showed Clay around

my property. Weaver came with us. I was especially, and, in a way, ludicrously, proud of my livestock.

"This is fantastic," said Clay when he saw my chickens and sheep. "Vermont has lost so much. The animals, what few there are, don't thrive. Our crops are meager. I left partly so I wouldn't take resources away from my family."

I didn't say anything. Weaver remained silent as well. We walked more of the land. I hadn't done that in a long time. It felt good to stride over all that grass and dirt. I had a thought to kick off my shoes, but we were walking a long way. Clay and Weaver seemed happy to be walking too. We had an amazing state. Verdant and rich. We saw rabbits running in fields. A distant coyote. Clay saw the rabbits, too, and whooped at the wonder of it.

"We have nothing like that in Vermont. Not anymore."

"We've got bears here," said Weaver. "Not a lot, but some. We kind of thought that maybe all the states still had wildlife on them."

"Nope," said Clay. "Some of the states are dying. They might not last much longer."

"That's sad," I said.

"Yes," said Clay. "Do you like it here?"

"It's my home," I said.

"I was hoping to go inland. Do you have cities here in Washington?"

"Some, but they aren't like they used to be. Mostly people too scared of the edge to live here. They think they'll fall off the world."

"They might," he said.

"You going to walk?" asked Weaver.

"Is there any other way?"

"There are horses," I said. "Someone might lend you one, if you ask real nice. Otherwise, we've been having some good weather lately. It'll be a nice walk for you. Long, but nice. I'll show you the way to go."

"Thanks," said Clay. "You've been very kind."

We returned to the house.

Weaver fell into a chair in the living room. I sat in another near him. We expected Clay to sit with us. Instead, he went into his room and returned with his small backpack.

"What?" said Weaver. "You aren't going *now*, are you?"

"No reason to wait," he said.

I could tell he thought it was much too boring to hang around with a couple of geezers. I wanted to feel offended but could not manage it.

"I'll put some food together for you," I said.

Weaver was irritated with him. "You just got here," he said. "What's your damn hurry?"

Clay had no answer. He looked at me, as if he wanted my help. I remembered when my son used to look at his father when I told him to do something he didn't want to do. Such an understanding, they had. His father sometimes helped him out, sometimes not. But the point was that they had something, some connection that seemed to be missing from me and my son. Now I felt a little of that with Clay. So strange. I wished he would stay in the house and help me with the chores. Do some work around the house. I'd cook for him.

I shook my head. Ridiculous thoughts.

"Let him go, Weaver," I said. "He's a young man. He needs to roam."

Clay's eyes softened toward me. A silent thanks that I appreciated.

A few minutes later he was gone. He waved to us as he rose over a hill, just before he disappeared on the other side.

Weaver shook his head. "That was completely disappointing," he said.

I nodded. "Still, it's nice to have someone new in the state."

Weaver turned from the hill, disgusted. He kicked at a stone. It flew off the ground and arced up to land near the house, then bounced once and hit the wood of the house with a dull thonk.

"Maybe that's enough for you," he said, "but it's damned little enough for me."

After He Left

I watched my son row across the sea. I didn't know where he was going and neither did he. We had been in calm waters for some time, so I was reasonably sure he would be safe for a while. How long was anyone's guess.

How can I describe my feeling at the time? It's hardly possible. My son was alive, I could see him, but it felt like he was dead. Who could survive for long without a state under their feet? And what were the chances of him getting to one before his food ran out? Before he left he explained how he would catch fish for his nourishment. He had devised a way to gather evaporated water from brine to quench his thirst. Oh yes, he had planned the thing very well, as well as anyone who had never been to sea might be able to plan it.

The current grabbed his craft and took him in a direction away from Washington. Forty-seven other states floated in the ocean. One of them was to be his new home.

For myself, I had to learn to live in my own state. I turned my back on the sea, walked away from the edge, and went inland. I lived in a small village and learned to be around people again. It was, I decided, a good way to spend one's life. I forgot about my husband and my son, as much as was possible. They still lived in my dreams and still haunted my memories, but I made them into small figures, to minimize the hurt that they could administer to my heart.

Was this easy? No. It was difficult. But we do many difficult things in order to survive.

Still, the years went by and the edge called to me again after my heartache had eased a little. I bid farewell to my new friends in the inland village and returned to my house near the edge. It had become rundown, of course, and needed a lot of care and work. I was only too happy to undertake it. The memories of my husband and son became happy ones. They haunted the house, and I turned them into amiable companions.

I was prepared to let things remain this way. I watched the horizon, and made my reports. Washington drifted down to the southern latitudes so we had balmy weather and pleasant breezes for many years. It was a good time to be alive, even if I was alone most of the time. Sometimes I traveled to the houses of other edge watchers. We would spend some time

                                          MARIO MILOSEVIC

together, but it was never comfortable. Edge watchers were not like the people I knew inland. They were awkward with company and always seemed like they wanted to retreat into themselves. Well, I could understand that. It's exactly what I wanted.

I had my animals. Caring for them filled most of my days. And I made a garden. In the evenings I had books to occupy me during the hours before bed. Mostly books from before the breakup. I liked the ones with pictures: seeing the world as it was then, the rivers filled with water instead of weeds. The cities with their amazing tall buildings. I knew the wreckage of Seattle, Vancouver, Olympia, and countless other cities remained in place, exactly where they had fallen, but who wanted to see those relics now? Much better to witness them as they had been, before the breakup.

I looked for land. The other states floating by because that was my job, my task. I saw them, occasionally, massive ghosts on the water, holding who knew what. Maybe robust populations. Maybe nothing but rats and weeds. But mostly I looked for him. For my son.

This Morning

Weaver went back to his house. I was alone again, which was a comfort in its way, but also a disappointment. Clay's visit was slipping from my memory. Had he really been here? It hardly seemed possible.

I fed the chickens, attended to the sheep. Circumstances change, but one thing always remains: the hunger of animals. It was the only thing that I could always count on.

Mid-morning a tall man arrived on horseback, coming at a fair trot over the rise. I was suspicious at first. None of the watchers have horses. Horses are for travel and we don't do much traveling. But the man looked to be no one dangerous or violent, as far as I could tell. I went out to greet him.

"You Susie?" he asked when I got closer. I had never met him before, but as soon as he spoke I knew he was. He was the voice on the phone. That clipped way of speaking. The condescending manner I could rely on.

"Who wants to know?" I asked.

He rode up close to me. Not so close that he crowded me but close enough to establish his dominance.

"I'm your boss," he said.

"Welcome to my world," I said.

"Where's the visitor?"

"Already gone inland. I'm surprised you didn't pass him. He went the way you came."

He looked around, then looked disgusted. "You should have kept him here."

"Why?"

"I needed to talk to him."

"You didn't tell me to hold him. Besides, he's bigger than me."

He looked backward, to the hill he had just came over. "I passed no one," he said.

Clay *was* a ghost, then? No. It just meant he took a different path.

"You'll probably be wanting to get back to the hunt," I said.

"*Search*," he corrected me. "I'm searching for him, not hunting him."

"As you say. Do you want to come in for some food before you go?"

My boss, the man I had never met before this morning, considered the offer with great seriousness. I could see he was hungry. People are like animals, after all. They need food constantly. It is what defines us, in a way, the need to consume. Without it we are nothing. Is that a good way to understand the world? Perhaps not, but it is *a* way.

"No," he said. "Thank you but no."

"At least get off your horse," I said. "Give him a rest."

"No," he said again. "I need to find the visitor."

"But why? What is so important about him?"

"He's not from here," said my boss. "He knows things."

I could see he was agitated. I recognized the discomfort. We all wanted to think the world was more than it was. But we were mistaken and always would be. The world doesn't hold more than we see or more than we can imagine.

Vermont was a dying state. Clay was almost the only thing left of it and Clay only wanted to live on Washington. At least for now.

My boss's eyes blazed. They longed for the old world, the one before the breakup. I had no idea the fire of the past burned in him like this.

"Come on," I said. "Let the past be, at least for a moment."

He slumped in his saddle, all the wind knocked out of him. I felt a tenderness toward him that I hardly knew was even possible for me.

He dismounted and stood on the ground next to me. Suddenly he seemed much more like a real person, like someone I could be friends with. We led his horse to a shady spot under a tree and I put out some water and hay for it. Then my boss and I went into the house for a nice meal.

"After we eat," I said, "I'll take you to the edge. Have you been there?"

"No," he said.

"You'll like it," I told him. "We can sit on the lip of the cliff, with our legs dangling over and watch the ocean. I never tire of that. The ocean is eternal. It'll always be there. And that's something to be grateful for."

Kim Antieau has written many novels, short stories, poems, and essays. Her work has appeared in numerous publications, both in print and online, including *The Magazine of Fantasy and Science Fiction, Asimov's SF, The Clinton Street Quarterly, The Journal of Mythic Arts, EarthFirst!, Alternet, Sage Woman,* and *Alfred Hitchcock's Mystery Magazine.* She was the founder, editor, and publisher of *Daughters of Nyx: A Magazine of Goddess Stories, Mythmaking, and Fairy Tales.* Her work has twice been short-listed for the James Tiptree Award and has appeared in many best-of-the-year anthologies. Critics have admired her "literary fearlessness" and her vivid language and imagination. Her first novel *The Jigsaw Woman* is a modern classic of feminist literature. She is also the author of a science fiction novel, *The Gaia Websters* and a contemporary tale set in the desert Southwest, *Church of the Old Mermaids.* Her other novels include *Her Frozen Wild, The Fish Wife,* and *Coyote Cowgirl. Broken Moon,* a novel for young adults, was a selection of the Junior Library Guild. She has also written other YA novels, including *Deathmark, The Blue Tail, Ruby's Imagine,* and *Mercy, Unbound.* Kim lives in the Pacific Northwest with her husband, writer Mario Milosevic. Learn more about Kim and her writing at www.kimantieau.com.

Mario Milosevic has appeared in *Asimov's SF, The Magazine of Fantasy and Science Fiction, Space and Time, Interzone, Alfred Hitchcock's Mystery Magazine, Pulphouse, Bewere the Night, Heroes and Heretics,* and many other anthologies and magazines. His poetry has appeared in dozens of magazines and in the anthology *Poets Against the War.* He has published three collections of poetry: *Animal Life, Fantasy Life,* and *Love Life.* NPR dramatized "When I Was," one of his most popular poems. His novels include *Claypot Dreamstance, The Last Giant, Terrastina and Mazolli,* and *The Coma Monologues.* Mario started writing when he was a young teenager. He submitted his first story to a magazine when he was fourteen years old. He didn't sell that one, but he hasn't stopped writing or submitting since. Mario has a particular fondness for short stories, considering them the ideal storytelling medium: short enough to read in one comfortable sitting, but long enough to convey the richness of life. Mario was born in Italy, grew up in Canada, and now lives with his wife, writer Kim Antieau in the Pacific Northwest of the United States where he has a day job at Green Snake Publishing and where he writes at night, on the weekends, and sometimes in his sleep. Learn more about Mario and his writing at mariowrites.com.

www.ingramcontent.com/pod-product-compliance
Lightning Source LLC
Chambersburg PA
CBHW050544190726

48284CB00003B/1202